"Devon, why are
so c

"You surprise me, Miss Kingsley," he replied with painful formality. "I thought you would have welcomed my distance."

"Welcomed it? Have you sustained a blow to the head, Devon? Why do you call me Miss Kingsley? I am Charlotte to you, and you are Devon to me. We are betrothed, are we not?"

Marwood breathed a heavy sigh and turned to face the woman who, in spite of her falseness, still had the power to tear at his heart. "Charlotte, let us not mince words. It is time we put an end to all this. I do not wish to be played for a fool any longer. I only hope you show a better face of it to your other gentleman."

"My...other gentleman? Devon, what are you talk—"

"You know damn well what I'm talking about, madam. I am talking about *Edward*."

Regency England: 1811-1820

"It was the best of times,
it was the worst of times...."

As George III languished in madness, the pampered and profligate Prince of Wales led the land in revelry and the elegant Beau Brummel set the style. Across the Channel, Napoleon continued to plot against the English until his final exile to St. Helena. Across the Atlantic, America renewed hostilities with an old adversary, declaring war on Britain in 1812. At home, Society glittered, love matches abounded and poets such as Lord Byron flourished. It was a time of heroes and villains, a time of unrelenting charm and gaiety, when entire fortunes were won or lost on a turn of the dice and reputation was all. A dazzling period that left its mark on two continents and whose very name became a byword for elegance and romance.

Books by Gail Whitiker

HARLEQUIN REGENCY ROMANCE
78—BITTERSWEET REVENGE
92—THE BLADE AND THE BATH MISS

LETTERS TO A LADY

Gail Whitiker

Harlequin Books

TORONTO • NEW YORK • LONDON
AMSTERDAM • PARIS • SYDNEY • HAMBURG
STOCKHOLM • ATHENS • TOKYO • MILAN
MADRID • WARSAW • BUDAPEST • AUCKLAND

To my good friend, Pamela Matheson,
who always found the time to listen, and still does

And to Brenda Chin, my special thanks

Published September 1993

ISBN 0-373-31206-7

LETTERS TO A LADY

PROLOGUE

THE GYPSY'S CARAVAN had not been easy to find.

It was tucked away amidst a dense grove of trees and set well back from the main area of the fair, and the two girls had stumbled upon it more by good luck than good management. They approached it now, apprehension and excitement on their faces.

"There, I told you we would find it," Laura whispered, her eyes fixed triumphantly on the canvas-covered wagon. "And you said it was all just a waste of time."

Charlotte studied the dilapidated caravan with an expression of thinly veiled scepticism. "I must have been mad to allow you to talk me into this. I cannot think why I did, other than to put an end to this non-sense about fortune-tellers once and for all."

"And I cannot understand why you are so sceptical, Charlotte," Laura complained. "You said yourself you would give anything to know when Edward was coming home!"

"I would," Charlotte grudgingly agreed. "But I hardly think a Gypsy is going to tell me more about my brother's whereabouts than anyone else has been able to."

Charlotte stared at the caravan with ever-increasing doubt, no more believing that Gypsies could divine the future than that evil spells and love charms could be cast by the light of the moon. As far as she was concerned, it was nothing more than hocus-pocus, a series of clever tricks to fool wide-eyed children. Certainly not worthy of consideration by a well-educated, sensible woman like herself.

Then why *had* she allowed herself to be dragged out into the middle of the forest for no apparent reason?

"Come to have your fortune told, have yer, dearie?"

The voice was unexpected, disembodied, and in spite of herself, Charlotte jumped. "Perhaps." She narrowed her gaze in the direction of the caravan. "I have been told that you have the gift."

There was silence for a moment, before a raspy voice replied, "I may, though it'll cost yer to find out."

Charlotte swallowed and glanced at Laura. "We've come prepared to pay."

A sudden movement at the side of the caravan startled Charlotte and she turned. There, leaning heavily on an ebony cane stood an old woman, her scrawny frame hidden under a shapeless black dress, with a shawl of bright red wool wrapped around her bony shoulders. She eyed Charlotte and Laura with a piercing black gaze, and then slowly nodded.

"Very well, come inside. But only you." She pointed one long, bony finger at Charlotte. "Since it is you who have come seeking me this day."

Charlotte glanced briefly at a wide-eyed Laura, whose speaking glance clearly said *I told you so,* and then walked across the glade, pretending an assurance she was far from feeling. She followed the Gypsy up the uneven stairs and through the narrow door.

Inside the caravan, there was little in the way of furnishings. Charlotte noted two rickety chairs, a small wooden table upon which stood a single white candle, bundles of old clothes and boxes of battered, smoke-blackened pots.

She lowered herself into the indicated chair, while the Gypsy lit the candle.

Gathering up her courage, she began, "I have come to ask about my—"

"I know why you have come." The reply was so quiet, yet so certain, that Charlotte's words faded into silence. She held her breath as the old woman sat down and fixed her gaze intently upon the candle, staring into the flame. At length the Gypsy spoke, her voice low and hypnotic in the silence of the tent.

"I see a man," she murmured. "A tall man, with hair as dark as the raven's wing. He will make you happy, this man, and he will make you sad. He will bring you the greatest joy you have ever known, and the greatest pain you have ever suffered. And he will do so in the name of love."

Puzzled, Charlotte asked, "Is this Edward of whom you speak?"

The Gypsy's eyes did not move. "His name is of no concern." She hesitated then, squinting beyond Charlotte into the darkness. "I see another man. Also tall, also dark. He loves you very much, but there is ... a distance between you."

Charlotte bit her lip in consternation. Could this be Edward?

"The ... first man," she asked warily. "Why does he ... bring me pain?"

"Beware the written word," the Gypsy intoned softly. "Anger and mistrust will follow in its wake. By love's hand shall you be condemned, and by the hand of another shall you yourself condemn."

Charlotte stared at the Gypsy in horrified fascination. Condemned by love's hand? What nonsense. Obviously, the old woman was making it all up, trying to frighten her with a series of preposterous mutterings. There could be no truth to what she was saying.

And yet, something in those strange, glowing eyes...

Abruptly, Charlotte rose. Dropping her coins on the table as though they were red-hot coals, she slipped out through the caravan door and walked away as though the devil himself were at her heels.

She left the fair that day, always to remember what the Gypsy had said. Always to remember that she had foretold the coming of two men, and the pain and joy that one of them would bring—never imagining for a moment that it might actually come to pass!

CHAPTER ONE

DEVON ROYCE, Earl of Marwood, glanced down at the exquisite emerald-and-diamond ring in his hand and allowed himself a brief moment of exultation. The ring, which had been worn by his mother, and by her mother's mother before that, had been in his family for generations. Until yesterday, it had remained safely locked away with the rest of the Marwood heirlooms, but now, it waited to assume its rightful place on the hand of the newest Countess of Marwood. For tomorrow, Devon intended to ask Miss Charlotte Kingsley to marry him, and he had no reason to suspect that the lady would not honour him with a favourable reply.

He glanced up as the library door opened. "Yes, Robertson?"

"Excuse me, my lord," the butler said. "Viscount Longworth is below and asks if he might have a moment of your time."

"Nicholas?" Marwood's smile broadened. "Yes, of course, show him up!"

Marwood shut the lid of the ring box and slipped it back into his desk. He was not even aware that Nicholas had returned to England. As an intelligence agent for the Crown, Longworth's comings and goings were effected without notice of any kind. Marwood's discovery now that his old friend was safely returned to

England once more was a source of considerable pleasure—and relief.

Moments later, the door opened again to admit a tall, dark-haired gentleman dressed in the height of fashion. Though he was a few years younger than Marwood, Longworth's handsome features bore the same stamp of good breeding and refined intellect as his host's. He advanced into the room, his hand outstretched in greeting. "Devon, I was hoping I'd find you in. How are you, old boy?"

"As fine as any man has a right to be." Marwood grasped the proffered hand and shook it warmly. "Dash, it's good to see you! When did you get back?"

"Early this morning," Longworth replied. "Very early, in fact. Came across by special arrangement."

"His Majesty's own?"

"None other."

The earl's well-shaped lips curled in a knowing smile. "Frenchies still on your trail?"

"Like hounds after a fox." Longworth laughed, his eyes crinkling with boyish charm. "Lost me rounding the last bend, though."

The two men smiled at each other in silent understanding. Having briefly been involved with the intelligence arm of the Crown himself, Marwood knew the risks inherent in fighting for his country at that level, battling an enemy far more dangerous than one armed merely with bayonet and sword. It was a war he might still have been fighting, had it not been for his father's unexpected death and the succession which had brought him home. As the 5th Earl of Marwood, Devon knew his responsibilities lay on English soil. But that had not prevented him from maintaining an active interest in what was going on.

"So," Marwood said, lifting the stopper from the decanter and pouring out two generous glasses of brandy. "I take it all went well?"

"Well enough, though I expect I shall have to go back once things cool down a bit." Longworth's reply was guarded. "There are few loose ends which need tying up."

"Loose ends?"

Seeing Longworth nod, Marwood grunted and silently recapped the decanter. He knew better than to ask. More to the point, he did not need to. "What about Lavinia?"

Longworth frowned. "As far as I know, she's still in Paris. We haven't been able to reach her since her husband was killed. Osborne thinks she has gone into hiding."

Marwood tapped his glass thoughtfully. "Has Osborne been able to find out what happened?"

"Not yet, though he has his suspicions. It's pretty hard to ignore the evidence."

Marwood drew a deep breath. "A leak."

It was not a question, and Longworth nodded. "I don't see how it could have been anything else. Obviously, someone discovered what François Duplesse was working on and decided to silence him. Fortunately, Lavinia was in the country at the time and Osborne was able to get a message to her urging her to leave. She got out just before the French arrived."

"And no one has heard from her since?"

"Just the one report, saying that she was safe, but not telling anyone where she was." The frustration in the younger man's voice was evident. "I wish to God she had left Paris while she still had the chance."

"She wouldn't, Nicholas. I tried to convince her to come back with me when I left, but she refused to leave François."

"I don't know why," Longworth muttered darkly. "It's not as if she'd been in love with her husband."

"No, but she was loyal to him, and even you cannot fault the lady for that."

"No, of course not," Longworth grudgingly admitted. "I just pray that she is all right. I suppose the fact that we haven't heard anything to the contrary has to be good news."

"I have always taken it for such," Marwood replied. "But you will let me know as soon as you hear anything."

Longworth chuckled. "Don't I always? You are probably the best informed ex-spy in the service. But enough of that. What's this I hear about you losing your heart at last. Is it true?"

Marwood's expression changed instantly. "Happily, it is. I have met the most wonderful girl. Beautiful, charming, graced with intelligence and wit, everything a man could desire. In fact," he continued, his smile broadening, "tomorrow afternoon, I intend to ask the young lady to marry me."

"By Jove!" Longworth exclaimed. "Never tell me that Devon Royce is actually to become riveted."

"The truth, from my own lips," Marwood replied with a smile.

"Dear me, I don't know if the ladies of London will ever recover," Longworth observed, shaking his head. "And what is the name of this most unfortunate young lady, if I may be so bold as to enquire?"

"Impertinent fellow! I would take you to task over that any other time, but as I find my stronger emotions somewhat tempered by the powers of love, I shall let it pass. The young lady is Miss Charlotte Kingsley." Marwood glanced at his friend and smiled. "Why the look of consternation, Nicholas? Are you perhaps acquainted with some deep, dark secret in my lady's past?"

Longworth raised an eyebrow in surprise. "As if any woman worthy of your consideration would be guilty of harbouring such a thing. Can't even say that I know the young lady personally, but dashed if the name isn't familiar. Has she a large family?"

"None to speak of. Charlotte's parents both died when she was young. She lives with an unmarried aunt."

"Kingsley, Kingsley." Longworth's brow furrowed. "I'm sure I know that name, though I cannot think from where." He shrugged as it continued to elude him. "Never mind, no doubt it will come to me directly. In the meantime, I am delighted to hear of your forthcoming betrothal. It is well past time you gave some thought to settling down and raising a family. Beget the requisite heir and all that. As a result, I have come to invite you to dinner in order that we may celebrate this most notable of occasions in the style to which it deserves."

Marwood grinned and tossed back the rest of his brandy. "No doubt it shall also serve to keep your mind off the fact that you are temporarily without a cook."

"My dear Marwood, how could you even think such a thing. I came here for no other reason than to enjoy the pleasure of your company after my perilous mission in France," Longworth sallied, adding, "however, now that you mention it, it did slip my mind that

I had given Mrs. Clarkson extra time off to see her sister in Kent."

"Yes, I thought as much," Marwood retorted. "Come, you shall pay dearly for your poor attempts at flattery, my friend. I shall order the very finest bottle of champagne with my dinner and enjoy it at your expense!"

"Dear me, I think perhaps I should have stayed in France," Longworth muttered, resolutely downing the contents of his own glass. "At least there, if I was fortunate enough to get out of a tap-room alive, it was with money in my pockets!"

"CHARLOTTE, would you be a dear and fetch some lavender from the garden? I completely forgot about the balm I promised to mix up for Lady Broughton." Catherine Harper flipped through the pages of her beloved, though somewhat battered, copy of *Arts Master-Piece, or, The Beautifying Part of Physick* by Dr. Nicholas Culpeper, and glanced across the room to where her niece was arranging a bowl of roses for the dining-room table. "Apparently, the rain has been playing havoc with her joints again, and she says that my balm is the only thing which affords her any relief." Miss Harper chewed gently on her lip. "She did complain about the fragrance being a little different the last time, though, and for the life of me, I cannot think why."

Charlotte endeavoured to keep a straight face as she carefully trimmed the thorns from a dewy, long-stemmed rose. It would not do to laugh. Aunt Kittie took her remedies very seriously. "No doubt it had something to do with the extra rosemary and the few drops of rose essence you put in, Aunt Kittie."

"Eh?"

"Do you not remember? You told me that you had cut back on the amount of lavender oil and increased the quantity of rosemary in order to make the balm more effective."

"Cut back on the... and increased the... did I, indeed?" Aunt Kittie glanced at her hastily scribbled notes thoughtfully. "Do you know, Charlotte, now that you mention it, I just might..."

There was a rustle of paper as she flipped back to the appropriate page and ran her finger down the list of ingredients. She snorted in a rather unladylike fashion. "Bother, of course that's what I did. I must have been thinking of the tonic I made up for Lady Harrington. That was the one which required the extra lavender." She ruefully shook her head. "Dear me, Charlotte, what would I do without you to keep me straight?"

"I daresay you should manage, Aunt," Charlotte replied fondly. She inserted the last of the roses into the vase and then stood back to regard her handiwork. "There, that will do nicely. What do you think?"

Aunt Kittie beamed her approval. "Oh, Charlotte, that looks lovely. You have definitely inherited my sister's flair for the artistic. Lord knows, I was never any good at arranging flowers or the like. Your mother despaired of me in that regard, and in a few others, I should imagine."

"Never mind, Aunt, you are far more talented at making use of flowers and plants than I could ever be," Charlotte replied truthfully. "Speaking of which, would you still like me to fetch that lavender for you?"

"Hmm? Oh, yes, go on then, dear. I can always use a little extra. No doubt Lady Harrington will be asking for some more of her tonic soon. I vow the woman bathes in it. You do remember where it is, don't you? Bottom left corner of the garden, just behind the sweet basil.''

Seeing her niece nod, Aunt Kittie adjusted the spectacles which were perched rather precariously on the end of her nose and returned her attention to the well-used book in her hand. "Now, have I forgotten anything else? I have the juniper, the rosemary and the white wax, though I may have to substitute something for the rose essence." She glanced at Charlotte over the rim of her glasses. "Do you think Lady Broughton will mind smelling of lemons this time, rather than roses?''

Charlotte laughed as she picked up her shawl and draped it around her shoulders. "I am sure she will not mind how she smells as long as the balm works. Have you seen my bonnet, Aunt Kittie?''

"Your bonnet? No dear, I haven't. When did you last use it?''

"This morning when I went to cut the roses. I thought I left it in here. Oh, well, I suppose it doesn't really matter," Charlotte said. "I shan't be in the sun long enough to produce a frightening amount of freckles.''

"Well, if you do, there is a wonderful recipe for mustard ointment here in the herbal. Now, where did I see that..."

Charlotte shook her head as she picked up the basket and headed out into the garden. Dear Aunt Kittie. While there was no denying that she was somewhat eccentric, it was also true that she was exceedingly popular with the members of the *beau monde*. There was hardly a lady in London who had not come to her aunt for something. Oil of cloves for toothache. Pimpernel water for the complexion. And her mustard plasters were said to be the finest available!

Charlotte finally located the patch of lavender and set her basket on the ground beside it. Sinking to her knees on the soft grass, she began to break off the stems and place them carefully in the basket so as not to damage either the leaves or the flowers. Aunt Kittie was most particular that her flowers not be bruised.

It was there Lord Marwood found her, her dark head bent over her work. He smiled to himself at the perfection of the heart-shaped face with its rose-dusted cheeks and sweetly curved lips. By God, she was a beauty! And obviously not expecting callers. "Good afternoon, Miss Kingsley."

Charlotte saw his shadow a moment before he spoke and glanced up at him in dismay. "Lord Marwood!" Her hand went immediately to her uncovered head in a futile attempt to smooth back the wispy tendrils of hair which had pulled loose of their pins. "Oh, dear, I had not expected, that is, I thought Aunt Kittie would have asked you to...wait," she finished lamely.

Marwood chuckled. "Your aunt was rather engrossed in a book when I arrived. I don't know that she even registered who she was telling to go out into the garden to find you."

Typical, Charlotte reflected ruefully. Once Kittie got her nose into Dr. Culpeper's book, one might as well be talking to the wall. "Dear Aunt Kittie," Charlotte sighed. "She is a sweet soul, though she does tend to become rather...distracted at times. I am sure if Mama were alive, she would have a fit at the kind of chaperonage I am receiving."

"She might wonder at the chaperonage, but I am sure she would be happy about everything else. Your aunt loves you very much."

"As I do her," Charlotte said indulgently. "She often asks me what she would do without me, but if the truth were known, I think I should be more lost without her than the other way round."

"And what of me, Miss Kingsley?" Marwood's voice was quiet. "Might I hope that you could come to care so deeply for me one day?"

Charlotte looked up at him with refreshing candour. "Do you not know me well enough, Lord Marwood, to know how much I have already come to care for you?"

Marwood heard the softness of his name on her lips and marvelled at the effect it had upon him. Never in his life had he been so captivated by a woman. Everything about Charlotte enchanted him—the softness of her voice, the music of her laughter... It was as much as he could do not to scoop her up into his arms and carry her off.

Instead, he forced himself to extend his hand and offer a polite "May I?"

Charlotte glanced up at him from beneath lowered lashes as she tentatively placed her hand in his. As always, his touch caused the strangest constriction in her throat. But then, it was hardly surprising that it should. Devon Royce was a commanding figure of a man. Tall, broad shouldered with well-muscled arms and a body kept fit by constant exercise, he was easily one of the most dashing gentlemen she had ever met. His thick black hair waved smoothly to the collar of his impeccably cut jacket, while his handsome face was lightly tanned from hours spent riding in the sun. He was a man who enjoyed life, and who took from it what he wanted.

Suddenly aware that she had been staring, Charlotte blushed and hastily averted her eyes. "Well, I suppose I had best take the lavender back to..."

"Miss Kingsley, a moment before you go. I would like to talk to you alone."

Charlotte felt her pulse quicken. "My lord, I really should be returning. My aunt—"

"Your aunt will not mind." Marwood's face creased in a knowing smile. "Apart from the fact that she probably won't even remember that I am out here, I don't think she will object when she discovers the nature of what I have come to say."

As Devon led her towards the stone bench by the fountain, Charlotte cast one last glance towards the back door. "My lord, I really think—"

"Miss Kingsley, do you intend to keep interrupting me the entire time I have you out here?" Marwood asked in some amusement.

"No, my lord. I was merely concerned about...Lady Broughton's balm."

"Lady Broughton's ba...? No, never mind, I don't think I want to know."

Charlotte valiantly hid her smile. "No, I am sure that you do not. Very well, my lord," she said, sitting down on the bench and placing the basket on the ground at her feet. "You now have my undivided attention."

"I am glad to hear it, because I think you know what I have come to say." Marwood sat down beside her and then hesitated. The delicate fragrance of lavender mingled with a seductive scent all her own went to his head like the most potent of wine, causing him to forget the carefully rehearsed words he had been about to say. "I

swear you bewitch me, Miss Kingsley. I have never
found myself at such a loss for words in the presence of
a woman before. Nor am I accustomed to having my
mind so filled with thoughts of your blue eyes that I
cannot see anything or anyone else.''

Charlotte bit her lip in an effort to hide her amusement, surprised to find the normally eloquent earl so
obviously ill at ease. ''Dear me, that does sound con-
fusing, my lord. Is there a cure for this affliction, do
you think?''

''I assure you there is, but I guarantee you will not
find a recipe for *this* in your aunt's book!''

Charlotte gasped a moment before his mouth came
down upon hers, silencing the words she had been about
to utter. She felt the strength of his arms as they closed
around her, drawing her ever closer to his heart until she
could feel the steady beating of it beneath his jacket.
She shivered as she felt Devon's fingers move upwards
along her throat and then cup her chin while his lips
pressed warm, intimate caresses against the tender curve
of her mouth.

When he eventually pulled away, Charlotte slowly
opened her eyes, tilting her face back so that she could
look up into his eyes. ''I see you gave up trying to find
the words,'' she said unsteadily.

Marwood's reply came in the form of a throaty
chuckle, his gaze resting pointedly on her lips, which
were rosy from his kiss. ''Some things are best said
without words, my dear, as you will come to discover.
Though what I am about to say cannot be said in any
other way.'' Devon's gaze grew suddenly serious. ''I
cannot tell you without words that I see your face in my
mind a hundred different times a day. I cannot explain
the emptiness that I feel whenever you are not with me,

nor the fulfilment I know when you are. I can only tell you that I find myself enchanted by you, and wish for nothing more than to say the words which are in my heart and to hear your answer as quickly as possible. Dearest Charlotte, will you marry me?''

Charlotte smiled. "Yes, Devon," she replied softly. "I should be very proud to be your wife."

Marwood caught his breath at the love he saw reflected in her eyes and, fighting the urge to sweep her into his arms again, slowly reached into his jacket. "This was my mother's ring," he told her quietly. "She wore it all the years of her married life. She gave it to me that I might see my wife wear it." He reverently slipped the ring onto Charlotte's finger. "I hope that you will wear it all the years of yours, with me." Lifting her hand, Marwood pressed a fervent kiss into the softly scented skin, his eyes meeting hers.

Unexpectedly, Charlotte felt the tremble of tears on her lashes. "Oh, Devon, I . . ."

The words stuck uselessly in her throat, but Marwood saw what she was trying to say. "I love you too, Charlotte," he whispered, before his lips came down on hers once again, capturing her mouth in a kiss that sealed his promise, and bound her to him forever.

CHAPTER TWO

THE NEWS of the engagement of the Earl of Marwood and Miss Charlotte Kingsley appeared in the *Times* before the end of the week, and as expected, Charlotte was showered with good wishes from her friends and relations. Laura Beaufort had been delighted by her long-time friend's remarkable good fortune, as well as by being asked to be a bridesmaid at what would no doubt be the wedding of the Season.

"Are you and Lord Marwood planning a long engagement?" Laura enquired as the two girls sat together in Charlotte's bedroom one afternoon, studying the latest bridal fashions from Paris.

Charlotte shook her head. "I shouldn't think so. Though we haven't yet set the date, neither of us sees much point in waiting."

"No, I don't suppose there is, once you have made up your mind to marry someone." Laura sighed enviously. "The Countess of Marwood. Oh, Lotte, you are so lucky. Your aunt must be thrilled."

"I don't know that Aunt Kittie thinks as much about the fact that I am marrying an earl, as that I am marrying the most handsome man she has ever met. She has already checked her tea-leaves and is predicting a long, happy marriage for me."

"She told me she was making a special perfume for you to use on your wedding night." Laura giggled. "One that will work like a love potion."

Charlotte's cheeks flushed a rosy pink as she quickly pulled forward a copy of *La Belle Assemblée*. She hardly needed a love potion. When Devon had kissed her in the garden, Charlotte had felt a fire spread through her body like molten flames as the intimacy of his kiss had deepened. It was a feeling she had never experienced before, and it startled her to know that something as simple as a kiss could spark such a wealth of emotions.

Unaware of the direction of her friend's thoughts, Laura glanced at the beautiful emerald-and-diamond ring on Charlotte's finger and sighed. "I just know it is going to be a beautiful wedding. If only Edward could be here to enjoy it with you. He would be so proud."

Charlotte paused, her smile fading at the mention of her brother's name. Dearest Edward. As a child, Charlotte had worshipped her handsome older brother, and when their parents had both perished in a fire, Edward had become her rock—the strength upon which she had survived. He was a part of her.

Some of her pain must have revealed itself in her eyes, for Laura impulsively laid a hand on Charlotte's arm. "Has there still been no news?"

Charlotte shook her head sadly. "No, nothing. No one seems to know where Edward is. There are no records of his mission, no reports as to where he was last seen. It is almost as though he had vanished."

"But surely someone must know something. What about Lord Marwood?" Laura enquired hopefully. "He has connections at court. Have you spoken with him about it?"

Charlotte sighed. "I haven't even told Lord Marwood that Edward exists."

Laura gazed at her in astonishment. "Do you mean that Lord Marwood doesn't know you have a brother?"

Charlotte hesitated for a moment. "Laura, what I am about to tell you is highly confidential. It must go no further than this room. Do you promise?"

Laura's eyes widened in alarm, but she quickly nodded. "I promise."

"About a year after Edward went away, Lord Osborne contacted me. From the war minister's office. He informed me that Edward was doing... specialized work. He went on to say that given the nature of my brother's assignment, and the fact that his exact whereabouts were unknown, it might be better if I did not volunteer too much information about him to people who did not already know him."

"Not volunteer information! Really, Charlotte, I do think Lord Osborne was being a trifle high-handed," Laura objected. "I mean, how can he expect you to suddenly deny the existence of a brother? What of the fact that you both bear the same last name, for example?"

Charlotte slowly shook her head. "Perhaps we no longer do, Laura. They may have given Edward a whole new identity, and that is something Lord Osborne would not have been at liberty to tell me."

Laura abruptly sat up. "Gracious, that could be exactly what they have done, Charlotte, and the reason why no one has been able to find Edward. I have just finished reading the most marvellous story in which the heroine was a spy. She was a princess, actually, but no one knew who she really was." Laura's eyes grew dreamy. "It was such a wonderful story. She fell in love with the count she had been engaged to kill, but who turned out to be the hero after all, and she married him. It was all dreadfully romantic."

"Yes, well, I am sure I do not find anything remotely romantic about this whole affair," Charlotte remarked more sharply than she intended. "All I want to hear is that Edward is alive, whatever his name is now."

"Yes, of course you do," Laura said, suitably chastised.

Glancing at her friend's downcast expression, Charlotte grimaced. "Oh, Laura, I am sorry, I did not mean to cut up at you like that. It's just that I am so desperate to hear news of Edward. Every day I check the post, hoping for a letter from him, telling me that he is coming home. That would make my happiness complete." Charlotte paused, her smile returning. "Still, if nothing else, at least I can draw comfort from the knowledge that he is alive."

Laura stared at her in bewilderment. "You know that? But how?"

"Because Edward and I were always very close that way, especially after our parents died. I would know in my heart if something had happened to him."

Charlotte sighed again, shutting her eyes against the tears which inevitably formed at the thought of her beloved brother. She could not bear the thought of him all alone out there in the remote French countryside. If, in fact, he was still in France. Given the nature of her brother's work, he might be almost anywhere.

"Well, at least you can draw comfort from the fact that Edward is still alive," Laura said, hoping to lift the mood of despondency which had settled upon them.

"And before the end of the year, you will be the Countess of Marwood. Is it not exciting, Lotte?"

Charlotte smiled her agreement. "Yes, of course it is, and I am terribly pleased. Now if I could only hear some good news about Edward, everything would be just perfect!"

AT MR. O'SHAUNESSY'S rooms in St. James's Street, at precisely eleven o'clock the following morning, Marwood lifted his steel and warily faced his opponent. The man opposite him was nearly as skilled a swordsman as he, and knew well how and when to strike. Not for a moment did Marwood dare relax his guard.

Cautiously, the two men circled each other, lightly poised to spring. Then, with the swiftness of a cat, Marwood lunged. Steel clashed against steel, and arms, well muscled from long hours of holding aloft the long, tapering foil, darted out and back.

Lunge! Parry! Riposte! Marwood deflected a parry, and then with the lightning speed for which he was known, lunged again, breaking through his opponent's defence and accurately pressing the protected tip of his foil against the reinforced pad on his opponent's chest for the fifth time.

"*Touché,* Longworth!" Marwood cried victoriously. "And my bout. That puts me three in the lead." Marwood removed his protective mask and grinned at his friend, aware that they were both breathing heavily. "Shall we call it?"

Longworth nodded and likewise removed his mask. His face beneath was bathed in sweat. "Damn you, Marwood!" Nicholas swore affably. "I'll get the better of you one day, though God knows when it will be. I swear you improve by the round."

The earl laughed and set his foil on the table provided outside the duelling area, where another two combatants had already moved in to take their positions. "The way you are going, it may not be long. Though I must say you were off stride today, my friend. I don't normally catch you out that easily. Anything wrong?"

Longworth set his own foil down next to Marwood's and shook his head absently. "Not really. Just a little tired."

Lord Marwood regarded the younger man knowingly. "At Barrymore's table again last night?" he enquired with a chuckle. "I hear he trounced you rather badly last week."

Longworth's hesitation was almost imperceptible. "Yes, he did. I thought the least I could do was make an effort to win it back."

"And did you?"

Longworth shook his head. "I fear I was no luckier than the last time. I shall have to try again next week, I suppose."

Surprisingly, Longworth's words were noticeably lacking in conviction, and it struck Marwood that his friend's tone did not ring true. But a quick glance at Longworth's face bore no evidence of anything amiss. Perhaps he was just being overly sensitive, Marwood reflected.

The two men changed their clothes and then strolled through the busy London streets towards their club, lingering there long enough to partake of a thoroughly enjoyable lunch in the pleasantly masculine ambience provided by a good gentlemen's club. That accomplished, they headed back to Marwood's residence in Grosvenor Square for some quiet conversation.

As they settled themselves in the library, Longworth accepted a glass of port from Robertson who, after setting the decanter and another glass on a tray beside the earl, left the two men to chat for a while about the latest news of the war. It seemed that things were going badly for Bonaparte. With Wellington's overwhelming rout of the French at Vittoria, the people's confidence was strengthened, and there was a renewed feeling that Britain would emerge victorious.

Marwood had seen a brief stint in that war. Operating undercover as Longworth did, he had quickly proven himself a valuable asset to His Majesty's forces. Indeed, Marwood sometimes regretted his return to civilian life and had, out of necessity, distanced himself from the service upon his return to England. Nevertheless, when Longworth had gone on to take his place, the two men had begun to meet in the privacy of Marwood's home to discuss what they could of the situation.

"I was not being completely honest with you earlier when I said that everything was all right," Longworth admitted. "It seems I shall be leaving again. There has been a development."

Marwood glanced at him sharply. "A little soon, isn't it? I thought Osborne wanted time to let the dust settle before he sent you back."

"I thought so, too, but it seems the nature of the business will not allow any delay. If Hornby had ordered my return, I might be a little more suspicious, but these were Osborne's direct orders."

Marwood nodded. Osborne was the same man he had reported to during his brief time in the service. A good man. Smart, shrewd and hard as nails when he had to be.

"Well, I'm sure Osborne would not risk sending you back unless he felt it was absolutely necessary." Marwood thoughtfully sipped his port. "It must be important."

"I haven't seen the orders yet, but I would imagine so. I shall be meeting with Osborne tomorrow. By all accounts, I should be away about a week." Longworth gave his friend a knowing glance. "Try to stay out of trouble while I'm gone, will you?"

Marwood grinned back at him wryly. "I shall do my best. By the by, I know things may be a bit up in the air over the next while, but any chance of your being in the country long enough to stand up as my groom's man?"

Longworth's smile widened. "Stand up with you? By Jove, dashed good of you to ask. Yes, of course. I would be honoured." He lifted his glass in a toast. "To Miss Kingsley. May the two of you know only happiness and contentment together."

Marwood raised his glass. "I cannot think that married to Charlotte I could know anything else, but I appreciate the sentiment all the same. Will you bring a guest?"

Longworth shook his head wistfully. "No. There is still only one lady in my heart, Dev, and at the moment she is hiding somewhere in France. Still," he said, glancing at his friend thoughtfully, "perhaps it is just as well that Lavinia not return before you are safely wed. I seem to remember her once commenting to me that you had a particularly fine seat."

"Did she, indeed?" Marwood chuckled appreciatively. "And what is wrong with a lady remarking upon my riding skills?"

"Nothing, except I don't recall you to have been astride your horse at the time!"

Marwood stared, and then threw back his head and laughed. "Well, you may rest assured, my friend, that as enchanting as Lavinia is, my eyes are firmly riveted on one Charlotte Kingsley. My only hope is that your own wedding will not be too long in coming, so that you may share in the joy which I myself have so recently discovered."

Nicholas raised his glass in another toast. "That, my friend, is a hope sincerely echoed by myself. And with God, the Frenchies and my dear Lavinia willing, one which I hope shall come to pass without too much delay!"

TWO LETTERS were smuggled out of France by special messenger later that same week, one to the personal attention of Lord Percival Osborne, Whitehall, the other to Miss Charlotte Kingsley, Green Street.

Charlotte's letter, when it arrived, was taken by Dickens and inserted between a number of other pieces of mail and placed on the silver salver in the hall. It sat there for almost an hour until Charlotte came in from the garden where she had been cutting flowers. Briefly stopping to pick up the small bundle of letters, she carried it, along with the basket of roses, into the sunny morning room. She had not looked at more than three letters, however, before she came to the one which had been specially delivered. The handwriting on the outside caused her stomach to clench. "Oh, my God. Edward?" she whispered incredulously.

Charlotte closed her eyes, painfully aware of the pounding of her heart. She had waited so long for this moment, but now that it was at hand, she was almost afraid to open the envelope. What if it contained bad news?

Finally casting aside whatever doubts she was suffering, Charlotte tore open the envelope and drew out the single sheet of paper. She took a deep breath and steeled herself to read the words. The message was brief, containing no more than a few lines, and she read it in seconds. Her eyes filled with tears, blurring the writing on the page. "Anna!" she called frantically. "Anna, are you there?"

The maid quickly appeared. "Yes, Miss Charlotte?"

"Please fetch my aunt at once!"

Wide-eyed, the maid skittered out of the room. Moments later, Charlotte heard the sound of her aunt's footsteps on the stairs. "Charlotte?"

"Aunt Kittie, come quickly!"

"Charlotte, whatever is the matter, child?" Aunt Kittie said, appearing in the doorway. She paused in dismay when she saw tears streaming down her niece's cheeks and a letter hanging limply from her fingers. "Oh, dear, is it...bad news?"

Charlotte glanced down at the letter again, and then back towards her aunt, hardly able to form the words. "It's...Edward."

Aunt Kittie drew in her breath and leaned heavily against the back of the nearest chair. "Edward! Is he...dead?"

Charlotte shook her head, filled with a lightness of spirit she had not felt in three long years. "No, Aunt Kittie. He's alive." Charlotte said breathlessly, ecstatically, "He's safe and he is coming home. *Edward* is coming home!"

LORD LONGWORTH set out for France the very day Charlotte received her brother's letter. During a brief meeting with Lord Osborne, Longworth had received his final instructions, and as a result, was better able to comprehend the importance of his mission, as well as the need for haste.

"'Tis no wonder Osborne was so anxious about this," Longworth said to Marwood as the two men sat together in the earl's closed carriage, heading for the coast. "We had thought the man long dead. Then, out of the blue, a message arrives from one of our chaps in Paris telling us that the fellow is alive and asking for our help in getting him out of France. The letter Osborne received today confirmed it."

"How long has he been missing?" Marwood asked.

"Almost a year."

"My God, the fact that he's still alive is nothing short of a miracle," Marwood said grimly. "Any idea what happened to him?

Longworth shrugged, the gesture almost hidden by the bulkiness of the black, multi-caped greatcoat. "We don't have a lot to go on, but from what little Osborne has been able to tell me, it seems that our fellow has been hiding out with a peasant family close to the Belgian border. By the sound of things, whatever information he has stumbled across is extremely valuable and Boney's men have been scouring the countryside for him. I'll give him his due, if he has been able to elude those devils all this time, he deserves to get out alive. He will meet with a quick and brutal end if Bonaparte's men get to him first."

"Who is he?" Marwood asked, intrigued.

"Don't know his real name," Longworth replied. "Goes by the code name Robin. I had heard rumours the last time I was abroad that Napoleon's henchmen were looking for an English bird, but I never connected the two."

"It is not surprising, considering the fact that Bonaparte's men are always looking for someone," Marwood pointed out. "Do you have to find this Robin, or will he be waiting your arrival?"

"No. Apparently he will be travelling to a point just outside Amiens and I'm to meet him there. Osborne feels the difficulty will be in getting him down to the coast undetected. There will be a boat harboured just west of Calais. If we make it that far, it should be clear sailing. Osborne has arranged for one of his other men to meet us at Dover and bring the Robin to London."

Marwood looked surprised. "You're not bringing him here yourself?"

"No, my mission stops at the coast," Longworth said quietly. "I have to carry on up to the north of England for a few days. All being well, I should be back about the middle of next week."

Marwood nodded, and the two men subsided into silence. Marwood was well aware of the danger to both Longworth's life and the life of the man he was being sent to find. "Damn, I wish I were going with you," he said unexpectedly. "This man is obviously of great value to Bonaparte, and there are going to be a lot of people looking for him. And for you, my friend."

"Probably," Longworth agreed with a slow smile. "But then, you and I didn't get into this game because we thought it was going to be easy, Dev, and neither did the Robin. The man has put his life on the line for his country any number of times during the past three years. It seems a small enough request to try to get him out in one piece now. You know you would feel exactly the same way if you were in my place."

Marwood smiled ruefully. "I already do feel the same way, and I'm not even in your place. Just be careful. Remember what I said about your being in my wedding."

Longworth laughed as the carriage slowed. He stretched out his hand, clasping Marwood's in a firm grip. "I remember. And don't worry—I intend to be there. I have waited too long to see Devon Royce shut up in the parson's pound to let Bonaparte keep me from the enjoyment of it."

The carriage came to a halt and Longworth glanced out into the darkness. He turned the collar of his black greatcoat up around his face, nearly obscuring it. "Right, I'm off," he said, opening the door. The smell of sea air assailed their nostrils. "Do not tarry here, my friend. The night is dangerous."

Marwood needed no further warning. "God be with you, Nicholas."

Longworth nodded, and then disappeared into the night. Closing the door behind him, Marwood sat back against the squabs for a few minutes before thumping the handle of his cane against the roof.

Whatever happened now, Longworth was on his own. It was up to him to find the Robin, and to bring him safely home. The future of England might well depend on it!

CHAPTER THREE

CHARLOTTE READ and re-read her brother's letter until
the words were engraved in her heart. It was short, no
more than a few lines in length, but to Charlotte, they
were the sweetest words she had ever seen:

> My dearest Charlotte,
> All is well, and expect to be home soon. Have
> missed you dreadfully. Pray tell no one of this.
>
> My love, as always,
> Edward

Expect to be home soon.

The words "no one" had been underlined and caused
Charlotte a certain amount of anguish. She'd had to tell
Aunt Kittie, of course. She could hardly be expected to
keep news like that from her own aunt. But how could
she not tell Devon that her brother was coming home?
She had not even been able to tell him about Edward's
existence. Now, not to be able to share the great joy his
letter had brought seemed even more frustrating.

But, knowing that Edward's welfare was yet at stake,
Charlotte willingly kept her silence, entreating Aunt
Kittie to do the same. Once her brother was home, they
would be able to tell everyone. For now, Edward's
safety was paramount.

When Marwood escorted Charlotte to Lady Harrington's soirée two nights later, he knew that something was not right. Charlotte was acting in a most peculiar manner. There was an air of distraction about her, a forced gaiety that was not at all natural. To Marwood, it seemed as though his fiancée were keeping a secret, something that she obviously preferred not to disclose.

"Charlotte," Marwood said after repeating the same question for the third time. "Are you feeling quite the thing this evening?"

"Yes, of course, my lord," Charlotte replied a little too quickly. Why would you ask?"

"Because I have just had cause to ask you the same question three times without once having had benefit of your answer," Marwood said indulgently. "Is it my question which is unexceptionable, or merely the manner in which I am phrasing it?"

Charlotte blushed self-consciously. "Neither, Devon. Pray forgive my lack of attention. It was simply that my mind was ... wandering."

"Your mind has been wandering a few times this evening," Marwood pointed out gently. "Are you sure you are well?"

"Perfectly." Charlotte belatedly gave Devon the full benefit of her attention, knowing that she had to. He was far too perceptive not to notice even the slightest change in her demeanour. He had already done so once, and Charlotte had no wish to compound her guilt by lying to him about the cause of it.

"Ah, Lord Marwood, Miss Kingsley, how pleased I am to see the two of you this evening," Lady Harrington said. "And may I offer my somewhat belated congratulations on your betrothal. I have not had opportunity to see either of you in person since the announcement was made. Have you set a date for the wedding?"

"Not yet, Lady Harrington," Marwood replied smoothly, "though we shall be doing so over the next few days."

Lady Harrington beamed her approval. "How delightful. You must both be very excited. I imagine some of your friends were rather taken aback by the news, Lord Marwood."

Marwood laughed easily. "Indeed, Lady Harrington. I fear most of them had begun to think me a confirmed bachelor."

"Hadn't we all?" Lady Harrington lightly tapped her fan against the lapels of his jacket. "I am only glad that I did not have a marriageable daughter casting her heart at you all this time. I know many of the other ladies who did, and they were in positive despair of your ever choosing a wife. But obviously all that was required was the right woman to come along to put such thoughts into your head. And clearly dear Charlotte was the one to do it. You are judged very fortunate, my dear, but then I'm sure you already know that." She waited expectantly. "Charlotte?"

Marwood turned towards his fiancée, dismayed to see that she was staring off into space, a strange, almost wistful smile hovering about her lips. She did not even appear to have heard the question put to her. Fortunately Lady Harrington did not seem in the least perturbed by Charlotte's preoccupation.

"Never mind, my lord, no doubt she is still a trifle overwhelmed by it all. I feel quite sure she will settle down, given a few more days. After all, it is not every day a girl becomes betrothed to the dashing Earl of Marwood, is it?''

It might as well have been, Marwood decided a little peevishly as Lady Harrington drifted away to mingle with her other guests. Wherever Charlotte's thoughts were, they were certainly not with him. Nor anywhere else in this room, for that matter. She was definitely distracted. Consequently, it hardly came as a surprise to him when, little more than an hour later, Charlotte expressed her desire to go home.

"You wish to leave already, Charlotte?" Marwood tried to ignore the niggling finger of doubt poking him. "But it is not at all late."

Charlotte gave him her most charming smile. "I know, but I confess I am a little tired, Devon, what with all these parties and celebrations in our honour. I had no idea it was such hard work being betrothed."

Marwood chuckled, his doubts assuaged. "I had thought you were made of sterner stuff, Miss Kingsley," he teased her. "I see I shall have to take very good care of you once we are wed."

Charlotte placed gentle fingers on his arm. "I certainly hope so, my lord."

As Devon went ahead to collect her wrap, Charlotte breathed a sigh of relief. In truth, she was not the least tired, but she was in a positive fidge to get home! She had no idea when Edward might arrive, and she desperately wanted to be there to greet him when he did.

By the time they arrived in Green Street, Aunt Kittie was just preparing to go up to bed. "Ah, there you are, my dears. Did you have a good time?"

"Yes, very good, Aunt." Charlotte's eyes darted anxiously around the hall, looking for signs of a new arrival. "How was *your* evening?"

"Quite uneventful," Aunt Kittie replied absently. "Though I did finally manage to beat Anna at cards. Dreadful girl has become quite sharp. Are you coming up, dear?"

Charlotte breathed an inward sigh of relief. Clearly, Edward had not yet arrived. "Yes, Aunt Kittie, I shall be there directly. You go on ahead."

"All right then. Good night, both."

When the sound of her aunt's footsteps died away, Charlotte turned back towards her fiancé. "Would you like anything before you go, my lord?" she whispered softly, moving into his arms.

Marwood smiled in a way that set Charlotte's pulse racing. "I would, but I fear it is not something your aunt would approve of, nor something I am likely to take in the darkness of a deserted hall." Devon lowered his head, his mouth covering hers in the possessive, demanding kiss she was beginning to know so well.

Charlotte moaned softly, marvelling that the feel of this man's mouth against hers could spark such a fiery response. She felt the warmth of his fingers through the thin material of her gown and pressed against him, aware of a fervent longing to be in his arms, to be fully his. She was astonished by the power of the emotions he roused in her. Was this what it was to truly be loved by a man? she wondered, savouring the headiness of the experience.

To her dismay, Marwood chuckled. "Mmm, what wicked thoughts are you entertaining, Charlotte?" he asked, drawing back and gazing down into her eyes.

"Nothing, my lord," Charlotte replied, flustered. "It is . . . but the heat of the evening air."

"Is it, indeed?" he remarked, enjoying the smooth feel of her skin under his palm, tempted to let his hands continue their pleasurable roaming. "Well, I shall leave allowing you to believe that, but I think we had best set a wedding date not too far distant," he said, well aware of the direction his own thoughts were taking. "I, for one, do not wish to wait any longer than is absolutely necessary."

Seeing no need for pretence, Charlotte gazed up into his dark eyes and shook her head. "No, Devon, nor do I. I want very much to be your wife. And as far as I am concerned, the sooner the better."

"Good," Marwood said with obvious satisfaction. "Then I shall call round tomorrow morning that we may set the date."

Charlotte gave him a brilliant smile, making him forget all his earlier misgivings. "Yes, and pray do not be too late," she said saucily.

Marwood pressed another long, lingering kiss against her lips before resolutely setting her away from him. "Rest assured I shall not be, my sweet. In fact, if I had my way, I would save us both a great deal of time and be waking up with you tomorrow morning."

"Devon!" Charlotte gasped.

"Good night, dear Charlotte." Marwood laughed and bowed himself out the door. "Sleep well, for tomorrow will be a busy day!"

Closing the door behind him, Charlotte smiled and headed for the stairs, hugging the knowledge of Devon's love close to her.

As she did, she had little way of knowing that at that very moment, two men were crossing the icy black waters of the English Channel en route to Dover. She had no way of knowing that one of those men was so weary that he could barely stand, and that it was only the thought of returning to England and of finally seeing

the beloved little sister he had left behind, which kept
him from collapsing altogether.

AT HALF-PAST ELEVEN the following morning, Marwood applied himself to the knocker at Charlotte's
door. It opened at once.

"Good morning, Dickens," Devon cheerfully greeted
the butler as he stepped into the hall. "Is Miss Kingsley
available?"

"Indeed, my lord." Dickens took the earl's hat and
gloves. "She is just having a word with Miss Harper in
the dining-room. If you would be good enough to await
her in the yellow salon, I shall tell her that you are
here."

He led the earl into the appointed room. "May I offer you some refreshment, my lord?"

Marwood shook his head. "Thank you, no, Dickens. I have but recently breakfasted. I shall content
myself to wait for Miss Kingsley."

Bowing himself out, Dickens closed the door, leaving Marwood to stroll about the room in a supremely
contented frame of mind. He was far too restless to sit.
Being a man used to athletic pursuits, Marwood found
the rather indolent approach to life favoured by the ton
decidedly untenable, especially when it came to the
practice of sitting in overcrowded drawing-rooms,
making aimless conversation with simpering girls or
dandies for hours on end.

For Charlotte, however, he would wait forever.

The earl glanced around him now, noting that while
the room was not as spacious as any of those in his
house in Grosvenor Square, it had been decorated with
just as much care and with an almost artistic elegance
due, he felt sure, to Charlotte's own unerring sense of

taste and refinement. The furnishings were of excellent quality. Marwood's glance took in the escritoire set against the far wall, and he strolled over to examine it more carefully. It was an exceptionally fine piece of workmanship, clearly late sixteenth century, and obviously used by Charlotte and her aunt for correspondence. Even now, a clutter of letters lay strewn over the top in a haphazard fashion.

Marwood recognized the invitation to Lady Rowallayne's ball, having received one himself, as well as a number of other notes and letters with pressed flowers and assorted fancy work in the corner, obviously from lady friends. But it was the letter tucked up into the corner of the escritoire—a letter which had obviously been folded and refolded countless number of times— which caught Marwood's eye. The signature at the bottom caused him to stop and take a second look.

"'My love, as always, Edward,'" Marwood read aloud.

Shedding all pretence of casual interest, Marwood picked up the letter and gazed at it carefully. It was written in a bold masculine script, and it was brief, no more than a few lines in length. It looked as though it had been penned in a hurry. It was addressed, "My dearest Charlotte."

My dearest Charlotte?

The intimate term of address startled Marwood. Charlotte was receiving letters from an unknown gentleman? No, it was impossible, Marwood assured himself, throwing the letter back onto the desk. The idea was preposterous. And yet, how could he deny the very proof which he had just held in his hand?

Marwood glanced over his shoulder towards the door, his brow furrowing as he tried to assess the importance of the information he had inadvertently stumbled upon. He was well aware that he was intruding upon Charlotte's privacy by reading her letter, but at the moment, her privacy was of secondary importance. If Charlotte, as his betrothed, was corresponding with another gentleman behind his back, Marwood wanted to know. It was his right, wasn't it?

Picking up the letter, Marwood read it through again, his eyes growing darker with each painful word.

"My dearest Charlotte. Have missed you dreadfully." Well, that was certainly clear enough, Marwood reflected grimly. The letter was from a man with whom Charlotte had once been close—perhaps a gentleman who meant a great deal to her!

"Pray tell no one of this." How could he misconstrue that? The fellow obviously felt the need for secrecy.

"My love as always, Edward." That was self-explanatory.

Marwood returned the letter to its resting place, all too aware of the jealousy suddenly gnawing at his insides. No wonder Charlotte had seemed preoccupied at Lady Harrington's soirée last evening. She probably hadn't wanted to be there at all! This letter had obviously just come into her possession, informing her that the writer was coming home. She had been reluctant to attend, knowing that he might arrive at any time.

And that was why she had been so eager to leave, Marwood reflected bitterly. Not because she was tired, but because she wanted to be here in the event he came to visit.

Marwood rested his hands on the desk, trying to come to terms with his confusion. Was he wrong about the letter? Lord knew, he wanted to give Charlotte the benefit of the doubt. Unfortunately, no matter how hard he tried, he could not forget how distracted Charlotte had been at Lady Harrington's last night. The memory of the soft smile on her lips twisted in his gut like a knife. That had not been the smile of an unhappy woman, he realized now, but the smile of a woman anticipating a much-awaited event, of looking forward to seeing something—or someone—very much. Someone she had not been willing to tell him about. And that hurt the most.

Five minutes later, Charlotte walked into the yellow salon only to find the room empty. Devon had already gone.

"DEVON?" Charlotte called, glancing about her in surprise. She stepped out into the hall. "Devon?"

"Can I help you, Miss Charlotte?" Dickens enquired.

"Dickens, you did say that Lord Marwood had arrived?"

"Yes, miss. I showed him into the salon."

"Did he seem in a hurry?"

"Not as I recall. In fact, his lordship seemed in very good spirits indeed."

"I see. Did he say why he left?"

"He left?" This time, even Dickens was incapable of hiding his surprise. "No, miss, he did not. In fact, I was not aware that he had. I have his hat and gloves here still."

"Really? How very odd," said Charlotte. "Thank you, Dickens."

Alone again, Charlotte tried to make some sense of what had happened. Devon had arrived, been shown into the salon, and then, barely five minutes later, had left again, without a word for her, leaving behind his hat and gloves. It was certainly very curious. And most unlike Devon. Whatever would have made him behave in such an inexplicable manner?

Charlotte walked back into the salon and sat down on the settee. Well, if Devon had left in such haste, it was entirely possible that he might return just as abruptly. Therefore, surely it behooved her to remain in the salon where she was.

Yes, of course it did. And it was with that comforting thought in mind that Charlotte glanced briefly at the ormolu clock, picked up her needlework and settled down to wait.

IN HIS STUDY at Grosvenor Square, Marwood angrily paced back and forth, his hands clasped behind his back, his jaw clenched as he tried to decide how best to handle this unexpected development.

Why had Charlotte not told him that she was already involved with someone? Marwood fumed silently. Would it not have been better than leading him down the garden path, making him believe that she was free to bestow her heart wherever she wished? Yes, it damn well would have been, Marwood cursed, struggling to bring his steadily increasing anger under control. He had thought Charlotte loved him. Yet now, as the truth came to light, it appeared that he been nothing more than a temporary diversion to fill her idle hours while she waited for this Edward fellow to come back. The letter he had found on the desk proved that. Or did it?

Marwood suddenly put a halt to his pacing. If Charlotte had been waiting for another man, why had she agreed to marry him? Could it be that Edward was nothing more than a former sweetheart of Charlotte's who had gone away and still thought her enamoured of him? Was it possible that Charlotte was not corresponding with the fellow, but that he had refused to stop writing to her? Good Lord, might it not even be possible that Charlotte herself had ended the relationship before the man had left for parts unknown, but that he had not been willing to accept her rejection?

That brought Marwood up short. Yes, it certainly was possible. In fact, any one, if not all of those assumptions could have been true. The more he thought about his beloved's sweet, trusting nature, the more he was inclined to think that he had gravely misjudged her.

There had to be more to this letter than he was aware of, and in all fairness, he owed it to Charlotte to give her the opportunity to explain herself. He might well be upset over nothing. Surely what he knew of Charlotte told him that she could not be unfaithful. Did he not owe her his trust in this, as in all things?

Angered that he had let his jealousy get the better of him, Marwood abruptly called for the carriage. He would drive back to Green Street immediately. Once there, he would straighten out this whole silly affair, and then he and Charlotte would set the date for their wedding, as they should have done this morning. With any luck, Charlotte would forgive him for his rudeness.

With even more luck, she would never come to know the full extent to which he had doubted her!

AT THE PRECISE MOMENT Marwood made his illuminating discovery, a gentleman was stepping down from the closed carriage which had pulled up to the front of the house in Green Street. His features were nearly indistinguishable; his forehead was hidden by the curly brimmed beaver hat pulled down low over his eyes, and his lower face was covered by the upturned collar of the heavy black greatcoat.

He stood for a moment and just gazed up at the house, a strange, almost wistful expression in his deep blue eyes.

The man opened the gate and slowly walked up the path to the front door. He reached tentatively for the knocker, hesitated, and then brought the heavy brass ornament down twice.

The sound seemed to reverberate through the house, and Charlotte, at that moment descending the stairs, halted at the sound. She could not explain what it was that told her this was not a routine call. She just knew. And as Dickens opened the door, Charlotte found herself holding her breath, her heart beating with painful intensity.

There was a moment's hesitation as the door swung open and the man glanced in. A flicker of recognition dawned in the blue eyes as they rested on the familiar features of the faithful servant.

"Good afternoon, Dickens," he said tentatively.

On the stairs, Charlotte pressed her hand against her mouth, muffling her cry. His voice was just the same, she realized dimly. Deeper perhaps than she remembered, but unmistakably his. As was the wavy dark hair, now lightly flecked with grey, and the brilliant blue eyes which were revealed as he slowly removed his beaver hat and handed it to the shocked butler. Charlotte's book slipped from her fingers and hit the floor with a thud.

The noise drew the man's attention. He glanced up to see a graceful figure dressed in a rose-coloured gown, poised at the bottom of the stairs, watching him. His chest tightened at the sight of her face. Surely this could not be the same coltish girl he remembered?

"Charlotte?"

Though his vision blurred, he was aware of the young woman calling his name, the sound of her voice cutting through the long years of darkness to touch something deep within his soul.

And then she was in his arms, calling his name through her tears. He caught her to him and spun her around, laughing and crying along with her. He stroked the dark, gleaming hair so like his own, and held her as though his very life depended on it, feeling the emptiness of the last three years fall away.

Edward Kingsley had come home!

CHAPTER FOUR

THE HOUSE appeared deserted when Marwood arrived; so much so that he had to knock twice before anyone arrived to answer his call. When the door was finally opened by a young maid, however, Marwood's left eyebrow rose expressively. "Is Dickens not about?"

Anna blushed painfully. "N-no, m' lord. He's in the kitchen . . . with Mrs. Bramble."

Marwood frowned. The butler in the kitchen with the cook, leaving a maid to open the door? How very odd. "Never mind." He handed the girl the second pair of York gloves and a beaver hat he had worn that day. "Is Miss Kingsley at home?"

"Yes, m' lord, in the garden. Shall I fetch her?"

"No, don't bother," Marwood said, warming to the idea of catching Charlotte in the very garden where he had proposed to her. "I know the way."

Striding through the house, Marwood rehearsed the words he intended to say. He had thought about them all the way over in the carriage. He realized now that he must have made a mistake. Charlotte would not deceive him. The fact that she had never so much as mentioned another man in her life should have told Devon all he needed to know.

Clearly, the letter was nothing more than the last desperate plea of a lovesick young man whose feelings for Charlotte had not been reciprocated. In fact, Mar-

wood could almost bring himself to feel sorry for the
poor fellow.

But when he stepped down into the garden and
caught a glimpse of Charlotte sitting on the stone
bench—with an unknown but obviously happy gentleman on the seat beside her—the words of apology
Marwood had prepared died instantly on his lips. Jealousy slashed viciously through his heart.

He abruptly drew back into the shadows of the house
and watched as Charlotte and her gentleman slowly
moved apart. It was obvious that while they were no
longer embracing, the man was reluctant to leave go of
her altogether and held on to one of her hands. Marwood could not hear what they were saying, but it was
clear there was a strong current of emotion between
them. He watched as Charlotte lifted one smooth white
hand to brush aside the lock of dark hair which had
fallen forward over the man's face.

The man seemed quite handsome, Marwood acknowledged, even though he did not have the benefit of
seeing him full face. What he could see was that his face
was lean and somewhat haggard looking. His clothes
did not fit particularly well, nor were they of the latest
mode, but neither of those shortcomings seemed to
bother Charlotte. Her eyes were glued to his face. Indeed, it seemed to Marwood that she hung on every
word. Words, Marwood acknowledged bitterly, he
would have given dearly to have heard.

But then, what did it matter? What did he need to
hear that his eyes had not already told him? He clearly
had not misunderstood the letter he had read earlier.
This, evidently, was the unknown Edward come home
at last.

Abruptly, Marwood turned on his heel. Gritting his teeth, he strode back through the silent house with a countenance as dark as a thundercloud. He encountered no one—which was probably just as well—and returned to the street where his coachman waited.

"Home, Evans," Marwood barked with uncharacteristic sharpness. "And don't waste any time about it!" He sprang into the cab and slammed the door shut behind him. Moments later, the horses set off at a brisk trot.

So, it was all true, Marwood reflected as he slumped back against the velvet cushions. Charlotte *was* involved with another man. More than that, she was in *love* with another man. He knew her too well to doubt what his own eyes had seen. Nor could he doubt the veracity of the letter he had stumbled upon.

There would be no wedding now. Charlotte would likely request a meeting, at which time she would make some feeble excuse about having made a mistake and then break off their betrothal. She would return his ring and wish him the best for his future. And Marwood, gentleman that he was, would turn, hat—and heart—in hand, and walk away.

"Like hell," Marwood swore softly. Charlotte might have played him for a gudgeon until now, but he was not going to allow her to continue.

The sooner this mockery of an engagement was brought to an end, the better it would be for all concerned!

BLISSFULLY UNAWARE of her fiancé's arrival and hasty departure, Charlotte studied her brother's tired face, with eyes that saw only that he was home.

"I can hardly believe that you are sitting here with me after all this time, Teddy," Charlotte whispered softly, as if by speaking too loud she might cause him to vanish into the mists again. "I was so afraid that I would never see you again."

"Now, Lotte, did you really think that I would leave you to fend for yourself?" Edward strove to keep his voice light. "What kind of brother would I have been to do that?"

Charlotte chuckled softly. "A perfectly normal one, I should think. I remember you saying once or twice when we were young that you wished I had been a boy rather than a girl."

Edward laughed and gave Charlotte an affectionate wink. "You never really believed that, did you?"

"I did at times," Charlotte retorted, her lips twitching. "Upon occasion, you could be very convincing. Especially when you were with your friends."

"Yes, well, I had to act the part in front of the other chaps, Lotte," Edward sallied. "Couldn't let them think that I was actually fond of my little sister, now could I? Not at all the thing."

Charlotte studied the face in front of her. It was still a handsome face, she reflected, with those startling blue eyes set above a firm jaw and a mobile, expressive mouth. His thick hair, a shade darker than Charlotte's, had long since grown out of any fashionable style and now fell in heavy waves around his face. Strangely enough, it only added to his attractiveness.

Charlotte smiled as she recalled the manner in which her friends had blushed and giggled whenever Edward was near. Especially Laura. Even as a girl, Laura had been painfully conscious of Charlotte's handsome older brother.

But there were lines around Edward's eyes and mouth that had not been there before, Charlotte noted sadly. Lines etched by grief and events which brought age to a man's face and a heaviness to his heart.

"Was it very bad for you these past three years?" Charlotte asked tentatively.

Edward glanced into his sister's trusting face and knew there was nothing he could say. She was so innocent. How could he tell her of the horrible things he had seen? How could he expect her to understand the violence that was war, the senseless killing and the wanton destruction that went along with it. How could he make her understand, when he barely understood it himself?

"It wasn't as bad for me as it was for some of the others, Lotte," Edward replied evasively. "I, at least, am here. Alive, and with all my limbs intact. There are many others who did not fare so well, I fear."

Charlotte bit her lip. She had heard stories of the war but she had tried not to listen to them. How could she, when she knew her own brother was out there fighting?

"How did you get out?" she asked softly.

Again, Edward's reply was purposely vague. "With the help of friends. After I got word to Paris telling them that I intended to make a dash for it, I learned of a family in the French countryside rumoured to be sympathetic to the English cause. I took a chance, and sheltered with them for a few weeks. I was lucky. Very lucky, in fact. They could just as easily have turned me in."

Charlotte shuddered at the thought. "But they did not, and now you are safely home." She glanced up at her brother with troubled blue eyes. "You're not going...away again, are you, Teddy?"

Edward shook his head and managed a convincing smile. At least in this, he could be honest with her. "No, Lotte, I'm not going away again. At least, not to France. Bonaparte spent a great deal of time looking for me. He will not be at all pleased when he learns that I have escaped."

Charlotte gazed at her brother in surprise. "How will he know that you have?"

Edward made a sound that could have been a laugh, or a sigh. "He'll know, Lotte. By this time next week, he will certainly know."

Charlotte nodded, and wisely refrained from asking more questions. She knew that Edward was not going to tell her anything about the past three years, and perhaps it was just as well. She didn't want to know how close she had come to losing him. She did not want to hear about the hardships he had endured, or about the awful things he had seen. All that mattered to her was that he was home, and that he could return to the life of a gentleman about Town. And she could think of no better place to start than with Devon. "Edward," she said shyly, "I have some news for you."

"Oh?" He heard the happiness in her voice and glanced at her shrewdly. "Good news, I take it?"

"The very best." Charlotte proudly held out her hand upon which sparkled the beautiful emerald-and-diamond ring. "I am betrothed."

"I say, Lotte, that's quite an eyeful," Edward replied, suitably impressed. "A wealthy gentleman, is he?"

"I would not care if he were a pauper, but yes, I suppose he is rather wealthy. I am engaged to the Earl of Marwood."

"Marwood? The name is familiar," Edward said quietly.

"I believe he was still the Viscount Rawley when you left. He succeeded to the title when his father died, just over three years ago. I am not surprised that you would know of him though. He is but a few years older than you."

Edward hesitated, abruptly changing his mind about what he had been about to say. He knew why the man's name had sounded so familiar to him. Just as he knew that it had nothing to do with the similarity in their ages.

"Yes, no doubt we encountered one another at some Society function or other," Edward replied in an off-hand manner. "And when is the happy event to take place?"

"We have not actually set the date yet," Charlotte confessed, recalling her fiancé's abrupt departure. "We were to have done so this morning, but Devon left rather unexpectedly."

"Well, when he calls again I should be delighted to make his acquaintance."

Charlotte blushed and nibbled at her bottom lip. "Yes, well, I am sure that will be a most interesting meeting, considering that Devon is not even aware you exist."

Edward glanced at her in astonishment. "I beg your pardon?"

Charlotte sighed. She had known this was going to be awkward. "I've never told Lord Marwood that I had a brother. You see, sometime after you went away, Lord Osborne came to see me."

Edward's smile faded. "Osborne came here? What the devil for?"

"To advise me in the strictest confidence that you were working for him. And to tell me that it might be better for all concerned if I did not talk too freely about you. Especially to strangers."

"Yes, I suppose I can understand that," Edward conceded grudgingly. "Given the nature of what I was doing, Osborne was probably concerned for your welfare. But it must have put you in a rather awkward position."

"It did for a while, especially with Devon," Charlotte admitted. "I so desperately wanted to tell him about you, Teddy, but I couldn't. I was afraid to. You see, Lord Osborne said that I should trust no one until he received word that you were safe, and as I had only just met Lord Marwood at the time, well, I really didn't know what to do, so I did nothing. I followed Lord Osborne's advice, and just kept hoping that you would come back. Then when I received your letter telling me that you were coming home, but that I was still to tell no one..."

Edward sighed. "My poor Charlotte. I never expected my work would have this kind of effect on your life. Indeed, I saw no reason why it should have *any* effect, and I am so sorry that it has. You know that I would never knowingly have put you at risk, don't you?"

Charlotte smiled up into her brother's worried face. "Of course I do, silly. After all, you had no way of knowing what was going on here in your absence. And I never did come to any harm. But I fear you are right when you said it made things a little bit difficult. However, all that is behind us now," Charlotte said happily. "Now, I shall be able to tell anyone I want that you are home, and the first person I intend to tell is Devon.

In fact, I shall send a note round asking him to call. I shall tell him I have a surprise.''

"Quite a surprise," Edward said with a chuckle.

"Yes, indeed. But at the moment," Charlotte continued, "I think you had best go up and see Aunt Kittie."

Edward grinned almost boyishly. "Do you think she will have stopped crying yet? I saw her ruin three handkerchiefs before she even went upstairs."

Charlotte laughed and gently squeezed his arm. "I am sure she has. She has missed you too, Teddy."

"Dear Aunt Kittie." Edward gave his sister a sidelong glance. "Does she still make those noxious remedies of hers?"

"More than ever. In fact, she has gained quite a reputation with the ladies of the ton for those noxious remedies, as you call them. Poor Mrs. Bramble has quite given up trying to oust Aunt Kittie from the kitchen when she's making up one of her famous elixirs."

Edward chuckled. "Bless her, she always was an Original. I'm looking forward to talking to her again. And to that end," Edward said, rising, "I suppose I had best make myself a touch more presentable. I wouldn't want her to think that an unkempt young gentleman had returned to take up residence in the house."

Charlotte rose with him. "She would never think such a thing. She has been longing for your return almost as much as I have."

Edward glanced round the familiar garden. A nerve jumped in his cheek. "It is good to be home, Lotte."

Charlotte heard the rough emotion in his voice and reached up to kiss his cheek. "It is good to have you home."

Edward tucked her arm into his as they headed back up to the house. "By the by, Lotte, I have neglected to tell you what a fetching little thing you have become over the past three years. I shall be rather proud to be seen walking such a lovely young lady up the aisle."

Charlotte squeezed his arm happily. "No prouder than I shall be to walk up it with you, Edward. I still cannot believe that you are actually home. I shall write in my diary that this is one of the happiest days of my life. Oh, I truly am in a fidge to tell Devon the news!"

To CHARLOTTE'S SURPRISE, Devon did not call round to see her that evening, nor did he stop in the following morning. She had risen early, fully expecting him to be at the house by ten, but when he still had not arrived by the time the clock in the hall chimed eleven, Charlotte began to wonder whether her letter had somehow gone astray.

"Are you sure you cannot wait any longer, Teddy?" Charlotte implored, seeing that her brother was dressed and ready to be off. "I am sure that Devon will be here any moment."

Edward, who was already looking better for having enjoyed a good night's sleep, regretfully shook his head. "Sorry, Lotte. I have to see Lord Osborne, and he is not a man who likes to be kept waiting."

Charlotte sighed. "No, I suppose he isn't, but I had so hoped you and Devon might have met before you went out. Oh, bother, I cannot think why he has not called. I did send a note round asking him to."

"I really wouldn't worry about it, Lotte, I'm sure we will meet up soon enough. Where are you off to this morning?"

Charlotte brightened. "Laura Beaufort and I are going to Madame Montpellier's in Oxford Street. There are two lovely bonnets in the window which I have been trying to make up my mind about and Laura has agreed to come along and give me her opinion."

Edward's mouth twitched. "Little Laura Beaufort looking at bonnets? My word, how things have changed. I remember her being a rather gangly girl, all arms and legs."

"Gangly?" Charlotte's eyes sparkled. "You may indeed be surprised at just how much things have changed, brother dear."

"Yes, no doubt I shall," Edward acknowledged drily. "Are you at home this evening?"

"No." Charlotte made a moue of disappointment. "Devon and I have been invited to Lady Stanhope's. One of her musicales, I'm afraid, and I did tell her we would attend." Pausing, Charlotte glanced up at her brother with a sudden look of hope. "But why don't you come with us, Teddy? I am sure Lady Stanhope would be delighted. And given the number of people that will be there, one more surely won't make any difference. Oh, do say you will come."

Edward shook his head gently. "Thank you, Lotte, but I don't think I am ready to face the rigours of a large gathering just yet. I should like a little time to acclimatize myself before venturing out into Society again. Besides, if you are going to be out, I shall make my own plans for dinner. There are one or two people I should like to see—on a more intimate level than would be provided by Lady Stanhope's musicale," Edward said quickly, seeing his sister about to interrupt again.

"Yes, well, Lady Stanhope's gatherings can tend to become rather crowded," Charlotte admitted, swallowing her disappointment. "Will you be late?"

"I may."

"Hmm. Well, I suppose there won't be much point in asking Devon to wait, either."

Seeing Charlotte's consternation, Edward flashed her a grin. "You really are anxious that I meet this sterling gentleman of yours, aren't you, poppet?"

"But of course." Charlotte looked up at him in surprise. "He is the most wonderful man I have ever met, and I can hardly wait for the two of you to become acquainted."

"Yes, I can see that. Well, I am sure we shall meet in the not too distant future. Right now, however, I must be off." He pressed an affectionate kiss against her cheek. "Have a good time this afternoon."

Charlotte smiled and watched her brother depart. She still found it hard to believe that he was actually home. Edward had been gone so long that she had to keep pinching herself to make sure she wasn't dreaming.

Moments later, she was distracted by the sound of an anxious knocking on the front door. "I imagine that will be Miss Beaufort," Charlotte said, heading into the parlour for her bonnet as Dickens came forward to open the door.

It was indeed Laura who stepped into the hall, looking quite the thing in a deep blue pelisse over a pretty new gown of blue-and-white muslin. A pair of sparkling blue eyes and a scattering of golden curls peeked out from under the brim of the matching bonnet.

"Charlotte? Charlotte, where—oh, there you are," Laura said as Charlotte emerged from the parlour, bonnet in hand. "Is it true, or are my eyes playing tricks on me?"

"Laura, what on earth is the matter?" Charlotte hurried forward. "You look as though you have seen a ghost."

"Perhaps I have, you tell me!" Laura said quickly. "Did I or did I not just see your brother driving away in a hackney?"

"Oh, thank heavens! I thought it was something quite dreadful," Charlotte breathed in relief. "Yes, that was indeed Edward. He came home yesterday afternoon."

"Oh, my dear Charlotte, how wonderful!" Laura exclaimed. "You must be so happy."

Charlotte's eyes glowed with contentment. "I am, Laura. In fact, for the first time in three years, I am blissfully happy. Edward is safely home, I am betrothed to a wonderful man and I am soon to be married. What more could I ask?" Charlotte turned towards the looking-glass. "All that remains for me to do is tell Devon the good news. I do wish he would get here. I have been waiting to see him all morning."

Laura glanced at her in surprise. "You have? How odd. I just passed him on my way here. I thought perhaps he was coming back from having seen you."

Charlotte's hands halted in mid-air, the bonnet poised a few inches above her freshly styled tresses. "You saw Devon?"

"Not more than ten minutes ago."

"And he was driving . . . away from here?"

"Yes, he looked to be heading in the direction of Mount Street."

"Really?" Charlotte paused thoughtfully. "How very strange."

Laura glanced at her friend anxiously. "Charlotte, you've not had a tiff with Lord Marwood, have you?"

"A tiff? Of course not." Charlotte laughed and lowered her bonnet. "I can hardly have had a tiff with a gentleman I haven't even seen. But I am surprised he has not called round. I sent him a letter last evening asking him to."

"Really? Well, I'm sure there is a perfectly good reason why he hasn't," Laura replied, her perpetually optimistic outlook returning. "Everyone knows how madly in love he is with you. Sally Chatsworth and Marianne Bradbourne were positively pea green with envy. I quite enjoyed watching them at Lady Teasdale's yesterday afternoon, trying to pretend that you hadn't made the most brilliant match of the Season."

Charlotte heard only a fraction of what Laura said, her mind lingering on her earlier remarks. Devon had been no more than ten minutes from the house, yet he had not called round? Why?

Well, there was no point in worrying about it, Charlotte decided, resolutely pulling on her gloves. No doubt there was a satisfactory explanation for all this, and one which Devon would easily explain. She refused to allow anything to dampen her happiness today.

A short time later, the ladies were comfortably settled in the pink-and-white chairs at Madame Montpellier's establishment, where Charlotte was trying to decide between the two bonnets *madame* had removed from the window. One had a wide brim trimmed with pale pink silk roses and a flowing pink ribbon, while the other sported a rather dashing feather which curled over the top and fastened to the bonnet with a pearl buckle.

"Laura? Which bonnet do you prefer?" Charlotte asked, turning her head this way and that to afford a better view of the silk roses.

Unfortunately, Laura, who had come along with the express purpose of providing an opinion on the matter now seemed more interested in talking about Edward than she did about hats. "Did your brother say where he has been all this time, or why he was not able to write?"

Charlotte replaced the flowered bonnet with the feathered one. "Actually he's told me almost nothing about the past three years, and to be quite honest, I don't expect that he will. From what I can gather, Edward would be just as happy to forget all about the war."

Laura wrinkled her nose. "Freddie Harrington won't even talk about it in mixed company. He says it is not fit talk for ladies." She picked up the two Kashmiri shawls she had been studying and glanced across at Charlotte shyly. "Is he well?"

Charlotte blinked. "Who? Freddie Harrington?"

"No, silly, your brother. I really did not see very much of him as he was driving away. How does he... appear to you?"

Charlotte stared into the looking-glass, seeing not her own reflection but an image of her brother's face as she had seen it yesterday. "Tired," she said quietly. "And certainly much thinner than I remember, though he seems to be fine otherwise. In fact, he looked much better this morning for having enjoyed a good night's sleep." Charlotte purposely did not mention the greyness of Edward's complexion, or the alarming way his bones seemed to protrude from beneath his shirt.

Laura nodded. "Yes, well, I am glad to hear that. From what little I did see of him, I thought he looked remarkably well. But then, he was always handsome."

Charlotte risked a quick glance at her friend, her lips twitching. "Why, Laura Beaufort, I do believe you are harbouring a tendre for my brother."

Laura's cheeks blushed a deeper pink than the material on the chair cushions. "I am not!" she replied defensively. "I was merely expressing an opinion. May a lady not express an opinion on a gentleman of her acquaintance?"

"She certainly may," a masculine voice observed from behind them, "especially when the opinion is such a flattering one."

CHAPTER FIVE

CHARLOTTE SPUN ROUND, her eyes widening in surprise. "Teddy! What in the world are you doing here? I thought you had gone to see Lord Osborne."

Edward smiled down at his sister in amusement. "I did, but as it turns out, I just missed him. He was unexpectedly called away."

"Well, how fortunate for us," Charlotte replied with a laugh. "Edward, you remember my good friend Miss Laura Beaufort?"

Edward turned towards the pretty young lady next to his sister, and raised one dark eyebrow in surprise. "Indeed, I do, though I am not sure I would have recognized her without your help. You do not bear much resemblance to the girl I remember, Miss Beaufort."

Laura blushed prettily and demurely lowered her eyes. "Why, thank you, Mr. Kingsley. And may I say what a pleasure it is to see you safely home again after all this time. Charlotte has been quite beside herself waiting for news of you."

Edward bowed in acknowledgement of the softly spoken sentiments and continued to watch Laura, finding her unexpected loveliness captivating. "I say, that's a fine piece of work," he remarked, noticing the two shawls she was still holding. He gently took the white shawl embroidered with blue trim from her. "And how well this one looks with the gown you have on. Better, I think, than the other.''

Laura glanced up at Edward shyly. ''I was just about to ask your sister for her opinion when you arrived, Mr. Kingsley. I am quite hopeless when it comes to making decisions on matters such as these.''

''I can well understand why,'' Edward replied gallantly, ''since no doubt everything you put on becomes you so well.''

Laura opened her mouth and then closed it again, suddenly rendered incapable of speech. Charlotte turned to regard her brother, a light of mischief dancing in her eyes. She had never heard Edward speak so eloquently to a young lady before, and certainly not to Laura.

But then, Laura had been too young to attract Edward's attention three years ago, Charlotte admitted. Laura had not even made her come-out before Edward had left for France, and she had certainly changed a great deal since then. She was no longer the gangly girl he remembered. Her figure had acquired graceful curves, and the childishly pretty face had matured so that it was now alluring in the extreme. That combined with a head of golden curls and the enviable perfection of a peaches-and-cream complexion were guaranteed to make any man look twice.

Yes, glancing at the two of them, Charlotte could not help but notice what a very attractive couple they made—he so dark, she so fair. They both looked so happy standing there, smiling at each other. It was also clear that neither of them knew what to say.

''Well, now that the matter of which shawl to buy has been decided,'' Charlotte interrupted, ''could someone please tell me which bonnet *I* should purchase, since that was our reason for coming here in the first place?''

Edward started and glanced at his sister sheepishly. ''Sorry, Lotte.'' He reluctantly turned away from Laura. ''Personally, I think the feather is much more elegant.''

Charlotte regarded her reflection doubtfully. ''Laura?''

Laura, who was still blushing from Edward's unexpected attention, not surprisingly echoed his sentiments. ''Oh, yes, Charlotte, the flowers are very pretty, but the feather does look—'' she smiled shyly at Edward ''—much more elegant on you.''

Madame Montpellier bustled forward. ''Has *mademoiselle* decided yet?''

Trying to hide her amusement, Charlotte removed the feathered bonnet from her head. ''Yes. I shall take them both, *madame*. While the feather seems to be carrying the weight of opinion, I do find myself rather drawn to the flowers.''

The sharp-eyed little Frenchwoman nodded and happily took both bonnets. ''*Merci, mademoiselle,* and may I say I think you 'ave made a wise decision. I myself would 'ave 'ad difficulty choosing between ze two. I shall 'ave zem boxed for you.''

As the cheerful woman hurried away, Charlotte put on her own bonnet and fastened the ribbons. In the midst of doing so, a marvellous idea suddenly occurred to her.

''Edward,'' she said, pulling on her soft, kid-leather gloves, ''I wonder if you would mind driving Laura home? I have just remembered an errand which I must attend to this afternoon, and Laura did tell me that she was expected home by three.''

Laura glanced at Charlotte in wide-eyed astonish-ment. "Charlotte, I never—"

"Yes, Laura, remember what you said to me just be-fore we set off?" Charlotte interrupted blithely. "You said that your mother was expecting you home early because your great-aunt Gertrude was coming to call. Is that not what she said?"

Charlotte arched one delicately shaped eyebrow and waited for Laura to catch on. Unfortunately, Laura who could be hopelessly naive at times, was still trying to fathom the reason behind this sudden change in plans when Edward tactfully cleared his throat. "It would give me great pleasure to drive you home, Miss Beau-fort, if that is amenable to you."

"There, you see, Laura," Charlotte spoke up brightly, "I told you Edward would not mind. After all I should hate to see you made late on my account."

Edward glanced at his sister slyly. "Yes, I'm sure you would."

Laura hesitated and glanced at Edward uncertainly aware that Charlotte was behaving in a most peculiar fashion. She had no idea what Charlotte was talking about. Was she trying to tell her, in some obscure way that she wanted time alone to meet Lord Marwood?

"Oh! Oh, I see, Charlotte. Yes, of course, how silly of me not to remember," Laura said, avoiding Ed-ward's gaze. "I *do* recall having told you that my great aunt Greta—"

"Gertrude."

Laura blushed. "Gertrude was...coming to call at...?"

"Three o'clock," Charlotte reminded her patiently.

"Yes. Three o'clock."

By now, Laura was totally flustered. Her cheeks were painfully flushed, and she made a great show of folding up the two shawls and putting them both back on the table. Charlotte looked at her in surprise. "Are you not going to take either shawl?"

Laura quickly shook her head. "No, really, it is quite all right. If you are eager to be gone, I would not want to delay you any longer. Nor do I wish to detain Mr. Kingsley if he is to drive me home." She glanced at Edward shyly. "Are you quite sure it is not inconveniencing you, sir?"

"Not in the least," Edward reassured her, hiding his enjoyment of the situation. "I have no plans for the next little while. In fact, perhaps you might like to drive around the Park before returning home. I am quite sure that your great-aunt . . . ?" He cast an amused glance towards his sister.

"Gertrude," Charlotte supplied helpfully.

"Yes, your great-aunt Gertrude would not mind if you were little late in arriving, would she, Miss Beaufort?"

"Well, no, I am sure she would not," said poor Laura, quite out of her depth.

Charlotte was delighted by the outcome of her scheme. "What a splendid idea, Teddy. How good of you to suggest it."

"Yes, I thought you might think so. Are you sure you would not like to join us?" he enquired politely.

"Heavens, no, you and Laura go on. I really must attend to this other matter as soon as possible," Charlotte fibbed cheerfully. "Have a lovely drive. I shall be fine. Brooks can escort me anywhere I need to go," she assured her brother.

The laughter in Charlotte's bright blue eyes told Edward all he needed to know. Laura had been a victim of the plot, rather than an accomplice to it. Not in the least regretful for his sister's meddling, however, he took care to hide his amusement. "Right, then I shall see you at home later. You will be home soon, I take it?"

"Oh, yes, right after I finish my errand," replied Charlotte sweetly. Edward nodded, and after having a quick word with Madame Montpellier, offered Laura his arm.

After the two of them had left, Charlotte turned back towards the mirror and smiled, well pleased with her machinations. How charming they looked together, and how sweetly they had gazed into each other's eyes. Exactly the way she and Devon had looked at each other when they had first started courting.

Charlotte paused, suddenly remembering the early, heady days of her courtship by Lord Marwood. It had taken little more than a glance from those deep, dark eyes of his to set her pulses racing. And when he had complimented her on how pretty she looked in a particular gown, she melted. Why should she not encourage Laura and her brother to feel that kind of happiness together?

After settling her business with Madame Montpellier, Charlotte rose and made her way outside to where Brooks waited with the carriage.

"Home, Miss Kingsley?" the young man enquired.

"No, take me to Hatchard's, if you please, Brooks," Charlotte said, aware of the need to pass some time. "I am of a mind to browse for a bit."

The young man nodded and set the pair of high-stepping blacks off in the direction of the popular bookshop. Not surprisingly, it was well attended this afternoon, and Charlotte encountered a number of acquaintances eager to talk about her upcoming nuptials. Being a subject close to her heart, she was only too pleased to respond. Once the pleasantries had been observed, however, Charlotte moved farther into the library, perusing the well-stocked shelves for some light reading material. She was so caught up in her study of the titles that it was a few minutes before she noticed Lord Marwood was standing at the end of the row watching her.

Her spirits lifted immeasurably. "Devon!" she exclaimed, rushing forward to greet him. "Where in the world have you been? I have been expecting you to come by the house."

"Have you, indeed?" Marwood greeted her quietly.

Charlotte completely missed the note of reserve in his voice. "Yes, of course. I've been in a positive fidge. I have so much to tell you. But before I begin, would you mind telling me what happened to you yesterday morning? Why did you leave the house so abruptly?"

"I apologize for that," Marwood replied briefly. "I suddenly recalled a matter which required my attention. I did not think you would be unduly concerned at my absence."

This time, Charlotte could not fail to miss the stiffness in his tone and hesitated, momentarily nonplussed by his polite but decidedly cool response. "I see. And why have you not been round to see me this morning? Did you not receive my note?"

"I received your note." Marwood's words were clipped. "I simply did not wish to respond to it."

"Not wish to respond? But—"

"I think that it would be better if we were to continue this outside," Marwood interrupted her, aware that a few people had turned in their direction and looked ready to approach. "I hardly think the middle of a crowded shop the appropriate place to discuss matters of a personal nature."

Charlotte glanced up at him in bewilderment. "Devon, what are you talking about? What personal matters do you wish to discuss? Has this something to do with the wedding?"

"Yes, you might say that," Marwood replied cryptically.

"Oh, good," Charlotte said in relief, "because I have something to tell you, too. Why don't you come back to the house with me and we can talk at leisure."

Marwood flinched at the happiness in her voice. "Perhaps it would be better if we took a drive," he suggested quietly. "I will not detain you long."

Charlotte glanced up at her fiancé and bit her lip. Something was very wrong. She hardly recognized the man who stood before her. The eyes which looked down at her were so cold that they could have belonged to a stranger.

"Very well, Devon," Charlotte replied meekly. "If that is your wish."

"It is."

Charlotte turned and preceded Devon through the library, willing her smile to remain on her lips. Behind her, Devon nodded politely but discouragingly to the people they passed. Once outside, however, Charlotte's smile faded. Marwood helped her into his carriage and then climbed in beside her, curtly directing his driver to take them to the Park. She noticed that he signalled Brooks to follow behind.

"Brooks is quite capable of finding his own way home, my lord," Charlotte said in an attempt at humour.

There was no amusement in Marwood's polite response. "I think it might be better if he followed."

They spoke not a word on the short drive to the Park. Charlotte, uncertain and confused by the anger she saw in Devon's eyes, refrained from speaking. She had never seen him in such a mood, and the intensity of it unnerved her. Once they had reached the Park, and had strolled a short distance from the carriages, Charlotte broke her silence. "Devon, what on earth is all this about? Why are you treating me so coldly?"

"You surprise me, Miss Kingsley," Marwood replied with painful formality. "I thought you would have welcomed my distance."

"Welcomed it? Have you sustained a blow to the head, Devon? You do not seem at all yourself today."

"I assure you, Miss Kingsley, that I am quite well."

"Are you? Then why do you persist in calling me Miss Kingsley? I am Charlotte to you, and you are Devon to me. We are betrothed, are we not?"

Marwood sighed and turned to face the woman who, in spite of her falseness, still had the power to tear at his heart. "Charlotte, let us not mince words. It is time we put an end to all this. Perhaps it is not happening exactly as you might have wished, but whether you tell me here or in the parlour of your home, the end result is the same. I do not wish to be played for a fool any longer."

"A fool?" Charlotte recoiled as though she had been struck.

"Yes, a fool," he replied tersely. "A cat's paw, a cuckold call it what you like."

"You will forgive me if I appear a little taken aback, my lord," Charlotte said quietly, "but truly, I have no idea of you are talking about. I have never played you for a fool, Devon. I love you!"

"Love?" Marwood spat out, unable to prevent the bitterness which crept into his voice. "Is this what you call love, Charlotte, for if it is, it is indeed a very poor definition of the word. I only hope you show a better face of it to your other gentleman."

"My...other gentleman? Devon, what are you talk—"

"You know damn well what I'm talking about, madam. I am talking about *Edward*." He stared down at her coldly. "Unless there is another lover in your life with whom I am not acquainted."

"Another...lover?" Charlotte stared at him in growing horror. "You are referring to Edward...as my lover?"

Marwood uttered a brief, harsh sound that could hardly be called a laugh. "I wonder if you are aware of the warmth in your voice when you speak of him, madam. Yes, I refer to Edward. What else would you have me call him?"

Charlotte did not answer, suddenly robbed of the ability for rational speech. She could not believe what Devon was accusing her of, any more than she could believe that the eyes she looked up into now were filled, not with love, but with a deep, unreasoning fury.

"Who told you about...Edward?" Charlotte whispered.

"No one told me, I saw him with my own eyes." Marwood's tone was brusque. "I saw the two of you together."

Charlotte looked stunned. "You did? When? Where?"

"In the garden at the house," Marwood replied in a flat, dead voice. "The afternoon we were to have set the date for the wedding."

Charlotte felt her heart give a lurch. "You came back?"

Marwood nodded grimly. "I wanted to talk to you after leaving that morning in what I feared was a rather precipitate manner."

"Yes, and so it was," Charlotte agreed readily enough. "What made you leave without even a word for me?"

"I found Edward's letter," Marwood informed her. "And I felt angry and betrayed when I learned that you were corresponding with a gentleman behind my back."

There was an ominous silence. "You read my letter?" A faint note of reproach crept into Charlotte's voice. "You took it upon yourself to read my personal correspondence without so much as a by-your-leave?"

"I did not take it upon myself," Marwood snapped irritably. "I was simply admiring the escritoire when I happened to see the letter lying on top of it. You had not taken any trouble to cover it, and as you *are* my fiancée, I saw no reason not to read something addressed to "my dearest Charlotte," and signed, "my love as always, Edward.""

"I see." Charlotte's voice was deceptively, dreadfully hushed. "So you read my letter and did not bother to ask me about it. You simply *assumed* that you knew what it referred to."

"I came back in the afternoon to ascertain *exactly* what it was all about," Marwood informed her stiffly. "After I left that morning, it occurred to me that I might have made an error, and that the gentleman with whom you were corresponding might, in fact, have been someone with whom you were once close, but were close no longer. I returned, hoping to hear you say that you no longer reciprocated his affection. But when I walked into the garden and saw the two of you together, it did not take long to realize that your fondness for each other was still very much alive.''

''I see,'' Charlotte replied coldly, aware that her feelings of shock and dismay were rapidly giving way to those of anger. ''So you read my letter and then spied on me in the garden, without making me aware of either incident. How gallant of you, sir.'' Charlotte's eyes flashed. ''Tell me, Lord Marwood, what do you intend to do next, now that my—'' she caught herself quickly ''—Edward is back?''

Marwood drew himself up. ''There is nothing for me to do. I assume that you would like to break off our betrothal as quickly and with as little fuss as possible. Was that not the reason for the letter you sent round, asking me to call?'' Marwood enquired mockingly. ''Did you not wish to tell me to my face that our engagement is at an end? Was that not to have been my *surprise?*''

Charlotte turned her back on him, unwilling to let him see the extent to which he had wounded her. She could not believe that Devon thought her capable of this. She was hurt more deeply than she ever thought possible, devastated to learn that the only man she had ever loved had condemned her without even asking to hear the truth from her own lips. How little he knew her that he could believe her capable of such deceit!

Turning back to face him, Charlotte slowly pulled the engagement ring from her finger and held it out, her face set, her eyes dry. She was too numb to cry. ''I expect you will want this back, my lord, since it appears that in your eyes, I no longer deserve to wear it."

Marwood took the ring, aware that Charlotte's face had gone deathly pale. "Have you nothing to say for yourself, Charlotte? Will you not tell me that I am wrong?"

Her eyes fixed on a point somewhere beyond his shoulder, Charlotte shook her head. "No, Lord Marwood, I will not tell you that you are wrong. Because whatever the truth of the matter, it has little bearing now. The damage is done. You have judged me and found me wanting. You did not give me the opportunity to defend myself—"

"I am giving you that opportunity now, damn it!" Marwood interrupted harshly. "If a mistake has been made, then tell me so that we may put this whole unfortunate incident behind us. Tell me that I am wrong, Charlotte, and it shall all be forgotten."

"Forgotten? No, I fear this will not soon be forgotten." Charlotte finally raised angry blue eyes to his. "A mistake has been made, but it is not one of my own making. You have already found me guilty of lying and now confront me with the details of my treachery. You did not come to me first and ask me to explain. You brought me here to tell me of your beliefs and to say that you now expect our betrothal to be at an end. Well, it is at an end, my lord. Not because of what you saw but because of what you believed me capable of. And that, Lord Marwood, is far more important to me than telling you the truth of the matter now."

Charlotte lowered her gaze, the eyes which had momentarily blazed with anger now clouded with pain. "I thought you loved me, Devon."

"I do love you, Charlotte!"

"No." The word was low and laced with sorrow. "If you truly loved me, you would never have believed me capable of such deceit."

"Charlotte, what are you talking about?" Marwood felt his own anger rising in the face of her maddening perversity. "I saw you in the arms of another man. I read his . . . his love letter to you. What was I supposed to believe?"

"You were supposed to believe that I loved you, Devon. You!" Charlotte flung back at him. "Not some gentleman in the garden."

"Charlotte—"

He reached out to touch her, but she quickly pulled away. "No, don't touch me—you have no right! I trusted you, Devon, and I thought you trusted me. I was to have been your wife—" Her voice broke, but she quickly collected herself. "You may indeed consider our betrothal at an end, Lord Marwood, and I hope it makes you happy."

"Charlotte, for God's sake—" Marwood began in total frustration. "Charlotte!"

But there was nothing more he could say. Charlotte turned and fled, running past his carriage and into her own. She slammed the door and instructed Brooks to take her home immediately, leaving Marwood to stand and stare as the carriage pulled away. He watched it until it disappeared from sight, and then glanced down at the ring in his hand.

He had never felt more angry and frustrated in his life.

BY THE TIME Lord Longworth returned from his travels to the north of England a few days later, Marwood had already departed for the country.

That had come as something of a surprise to Long-worth. He had been looking forward to seeing Mar-wood again and to hearing news of Miss Kingsley's joyful reunion with her brother—the very man Long-worth had been sent to France to rescue. To learn that the prospective bridegroom had taken himself off to the country was curious, to say the least.

To that end, Longworth drove his sporty high-perch phaeton towards the second of his two intended desti-nations that afternoon and pulled up shortly thereafter at the Kingsley residence in Green Street. Edward had given him the address before they had parted company at Dover, and now that his mission was concluded, Longworth was eager to see how Kingsley was settling back into his old life.

After paying a young lad a farthing to hold the horses, Nicholas climbed the front steps and knocked on the door.

Charlotte, sitting with Aunt Kittie in the yellow sa-lon, heard the knock and stiffened, wondering, as she did every time Dickens greeted a caller, whether it might be Lord Marwood come to see her.

Since their tempestuous meeting in the Park, she had heard nothing from Devon. She was not even sure that he was in Town, so complete was the silence. Rumour had it that he had left for his country house, though no one seemed to be sure.

Not that it mattered, Charlotte assured herself. She was still too angry over the discovery of his inexcusable lack of trust to consider forgiving him. She was only thankful that she had found out the truth of his suspi-cious nature *before* they were joined in matrimony rather than after.

"Excuse me, Miss Kingsley," Dickens said, "but Lord Longworth has called."

"Lord Longworth?" Charlotte glanced at her aunt in surprise. "But he is one of Devon's friends. I wonder why he would be calling to see me?"

"Perhaps he has news of Lord Marwood," Aunt Kittie said hopefully, aware that a rift had sprung up between her niece and the dashing earl, though not of the reason why.

Charlotte stiffened. "If he has, I have no wish to hear it. What Lord Marwood does is of no concern to me, Aunt."

"Well, I should like to hear news of him," Aunt Kittie said, displaying her usual determination. "Show him in, Dickens, and be so good as to bring refreshments. No doubt the gentleman would enjoy a glass of my special elderberry wine."

"Very good, Miss Harper."

In a moment, Lord Longworth appeared in the doorway. Charlotte's aunt graciously rose to greet him. "Good afternoon, Lord Longworth, I am Catherine Harper."

"Miss Harper, I hope I find you well?" Nicholas said, bowing over the lady's hand.

"Very well indeed, my lord. May I introduce my niece, Miss Charlotte Kingsley."

Longworth turned towards Charlotte, immediately understanding the reason for Marwood's devotion towards her. Apart from her obvious loveliness, there was a quiet dignity and gentleness about Charlotte Kingsley that any man would find appealing. "Miss Kingsley, may I say what a pleasure it is to finally meet you. Lord Marwood has spoken of you often."

Charlotte quickly lowered her lashes, masking the expression in her eyes. "It is kind of you to say so, Lord Longworth. Won't you sit down?"

"How is it we have not seen you before, Lord Longworth?" Aunt Kittie asked. "I understand you are a great friend of the earl's."

Charlotte sighed. Aunt Kittie was nothing if not direct. Fortunately, Lord Longworth seemed to take her aunt's quizzing in his stride. "Indeed I am, Miss Harper, but I have been out of London a good deal lately on business." Longworth sat down in an elegant wing-backed chair and smiled at Charlotte cordially. "In fact, I am only just this morning returned to London, or I would have come earlier to extend my felicitations on your betrothal and forthcoming marriage."

An awkward silence descended upon the room. Charlotte felt her cheeks burn. "I fear you are... misinformed, Lord Longworth," she replied quietly. "There is to be no marriage."

Longworth glanced at her in astonishment. "But there must be some mistake! Before I left London, Lord Marwood gave me to understand—"

"Things have... changed since you left London, my lord," Charlotte interrupted. "Lord Marwood and I are... no longer betrothed."

Longworth heard the slight hesitation in her voice. "No longer betrothed?" he repeated, his voice gently questioning. When Charlotte did not reply, Longworth risked a quick glance at Miss Harper and saw her shake her head sadly. He saw the regret in her eyes, and did not delve any further.

"I see." Longworth hesitated a fraction longer before offering the apology he knew was due. "Forgive me, Miss Kingsley, I did not mean to cause you any embarrassment. I hope you did not take offence at my words."

"No apology is necessary, Lord Longworth, nor has offence been taken," Charlotte replied in a quietly composed voice. "As you said, you have been...away. You could not be expected to know."

"No, of course not."

Longworth studied the averted face of the woman in front of him, and saw far more than just the composed front she showed to others. He saw a young woman who was desperately close to tears and trying very hard not to show it. And he began to wonder more than ever why his best friend, supposedly head over heels in love with this young woman, had left Town without a word.

Charlotte, however, in an effort to be polite, forced a smile to her lips. "But come, Lord Longworth, it is a poor face we are showing you on your return to London. You say that you have been away. Perhaps you will regale us with tales of your adventures."

"I hardly think you would be interested in such things, Miss Kingsley," Longworth replied with a casually deceptive grimace. "They were not at all noteworthy."

"Indeed, Lotte," another masculine voice said unexpectedly from the doorway. "From what I hear, Lord Longworth's travels were about as interesting as a month-long stay in Brighton."

Charlotte, who had been unaware of her brother's silent arrival, gave a start and then laughed somewhat self-consciously. "Edward, I swear you move about more silently than a ghost! I did not even hear you come in."

Edward laughed and ruffled her dark curls affectionately. "A little trick I learned, Lotte. Nothing to be concerned about, though it does come in handy upon occasion."

"Yes, I am sure it does," Charlotte agreed dubiously. She glanced from her brother to Lord Longworth with a questioning smile. "And how is it that you come to know where Lord Longworth has been? Am I to understand that the two of you are already acquainted?"

"Happened we met at the club for lunch. Isn't that right, Longworth?" Edward said smoothly.

"Yes, indeed. Chatted for well over an hour," came the equally smooth reply. "And I fear your brother is quite correct, Miss Kingsley," Longworth admitted. "My travels were prosaic, at best, and certainly not worthy of discussion here. In fact, it was actually your brother I came to see." He levelled a meaningful glance at Edward. "I managed to get appointments for us at Gentleman Jackson's rooms. I thought you might appreciate a little exercise."

One of Edward's dark eyebrows lifted in silent understanding. "Yes, I would. Very much," he replied softly. "Good of you to take the trouble."

"Not in the least," said Longworth, rising. "And to that end, we had best be on our way."

Aunt Kittie glanced up in dismay. "Oh, Edward, must you leave so soon? Our guest has not even had time to sample my elderberry wine." She winked at the viscount mischievously. "You really should try some, Lord Longworth. It was a particularly good crop of berries this year."

Longworth smiled, but regretfully shook his head. "Unfortunately, I must decline your hospitality this time, Miss Harper." He glanced pointedly at Edward. "I'm afraid we must be going."

It seemed to Charlotte that a great deal was being left unsaid, and she began to wonder whether Lord Longworth might somehow be involved in Edward's line of work. As quickly as the thought came, however, Charlotte dismissed it. She was not at all sure that she even wanted to know. Accordingly, she rose and accompanied her brother and Lord Longworth to the door.

"It was a pleasure meeting you, Lord Longworth," Charlotte said quietly, then added, as Edward turned away to speak to Aunt Kittie, "and allow me to apologize again for the...awkwardness you encountered earlier."

Longworth did not miss Charlotte's quick glance towards her brother and lifted an eyebrow in surprise. Obviously, Edward Kingsley was not yet aware that his sister's betrothal was at an end, and for whatever reason, Charlotte wanted it kept that way.

He bowed eloquently, every inch the gentleman. "There is no need to apologize, Miss Kingsley. It is I who spoke out of turn, and I who crave your forgiveness."

Charlotte nodded. "Thank you, my lord."

"I hope we shall see you again, Lord Longworth," Aunt Kittie said as he turned to leave. "And perhaps next time, you will stay longer," she added meaningfully.

Longworth's smile was unaffected. "It would be my pleasure, Miss Harper. I admit to having a fondness for good elderberry wine."

Edward dropped a quick kiss on Charlotte's cheek before following Longworth out. "I may be late this evening, Lotte, so you needn't bother waiting up. I'll see you in the morning."

No, she wouldn't wait up, Charlotte thought, slowly returning to her chair after her brother and Lord Longworth had departed. The past few nights she had gone to bed very early, not seeing any reason for staying up.

She could not imagine that there would be any better reason for staying up late tonight, either.

CHAPTER SIX

NOT SURPRISINGLY, like Charlotte, Marwood was finding his own nights annoyingly restless. His sleep, indeed his very dreams, were filled with images of Charlotte's face. A face which, more often than not, was dampened by salty tears, and which gazed up at him with dark, accusing eyes.

Marwood sighed and abruptly pulled his stallion to a halt at the crest of the hill. He had thought the country the best place for him to cool his heels and to come to terms with the painful reality of his situation with Charlotte. He had hoped that it might have afforded him some release from the turmoil that burned in his gut.

And yet, as he gazed out over the gently rolling hills of his Cotswolds estate, Marwood began to suspect that it was a futile exercise at best. Even here, where there was nothing to give a man cause for aggravation, he could find no peace. He could not forget the woman who had become the single most important thing in his life. And worse, he could not forget the way Charlotte had looked at him.

She had been shocked by his accusation, Marwood realized now, staring blindly at the endless green fields. Stunned by his accusation that she was involved with another man. Contrary to what he had expected, Charlotte had not seemed at all relieved by his willingness to let her go. She had appeared totally devastated by it.

But how could that be, he asked himself for the hundredth time. He had seen her with another man, hadn't he? He had read the letter. What more did he need to convince himself that she was guilty?

Nothing. He needed to hear nothing from Charlotte, nor did he expect to. There had been no communication between them since that day she had run from him in the Park.

Well, so be it, Marwood decided grimly, turning the stallion back in the direction of Marwood Hall. There was nothing he could do now but head back to London and try to pick up the threads of his life. There were other women wishing to be the Countess of Marwood. He would take his pick of them.

But not now. Maybe next year. Or the year after that. Or perhaps in a hundred years when the memory of Charlotte's love had finally faded into oblivion.

NOT MORE THAN two hours after Marwood's return to London, Lord Longworth arrived. "Afternoon, Dev," Longworth said as Robertson showed him into the library.

"Longworth, you're back." Marwood greeted his friend with as much enthusiasm as he could muster. "I hadn't expected to see you so soon. Accomplish your mission?"

"I accomplished mine," Longworth replied. "What the devil happened to yours?"

Marwood methodically poured two glasses of brandy and handed one to his friend. "My mission? I am not sure I follow you."

"Come on, Dev, you know what I'm talking about."
Longworth's voice softened. "I have been to see Miss
Kingsley."

Marwood raised the glass to his lips, carefully ob-
serving his friend over the rim. "Have you? And what
did you find?"

"I found a lady who was very upset and trying hard
not to show it. Especially after I made a fool of myself
by offering my felicitations on your betrothal!"

Marwood sighed and tossed back the rest of his
drink. "Yes, my betrothal. The briefest one, no doubt,
in history."

Longworth looked at him askance. "So what happened? I know you proposed to her."

"Yes, I proposed to her."

"And?" Longworth prompted.

"And she accepted."

"And?"

"And nothing. She . . . broke it off."

"*She* broke it off?" Longworth said incredulously.
"You're telling me that Miss Kingsley broke off your
betrothal?"

"Yes. Because if she hadn't, I would have," Marwood was stung into replying.

"You would have—Devon, what the devil is going
on?" Longworth demanded. "You told me that you
were in love with the woman. What happened to make
you change your mind?"

"Nothing."

"Nothing?" Longworth scoffed. "Try again, Dev, I
don't believe you."

"Damn it, Nicholas, leave it alone!" Marwood
growled. "This is none of your affair."

"It bloody well is my affair," Longworth asserted. "You're my best friend, and I want to know why one minute you can't get enough of the woman and the next you're trying to put as much distance between the two of you as possible."

"I am not trying to put distance between us," Marwood replied bitterly. "Charlotte simply doesn't need me anymore. She has...Edward," he muttered darkly.

"Edward?" The surprise in Longworth's voice was unmistakable. "What has Edward to do with this?"

Marwood nearly dropped his glass. "You know Edward?"

"Know him? I damn well should know him," Longworth replied flatly. "I just about got myself killed getting him out of France."

The silence was so long that it seemed to stretch into the next century. "Edward is...the Robin?" Marwood asked incredulously.

"Yes, of course. Didn't you know?"

"How in blazes was I supposed to know?" Marwood snapped. "You have only just told me."

"Damn it man, I know that, but I thought Edward would have told you himself. Or Charlotte, when you went to see them."

"Them? You thought I would have gone to see them?" Marwood's eyes glinted like chips of black granite. "Your sense of chivalry is somewhat misplaced, Nicholas. The next thing you'll be saying is that I should have extended my heartfelt congratulations on their reunion."

"Well, yes, of course you should have." Longworth glanced at his friend in surprise. "You mean you did not?"

Marwood's countenance darkened so forebodingly that even Longworth flinched. "No, obviously you did not," Longworth muttered quickly. "Though why you did not, I cannot imagine. It isn't every day a girl's brother returns from the wars a hero, especially a brother who has been presumed dead for the past eight months."

Marwood stared at his friend in utter stupefaction. "Her brother? *Charlotte's* brother? What the devil are you talking about, Longworth? Charlotte doesn't have a brother. At least not one that she has ever mentioned to me."

"No, very likely she did not mention him," Longworth agreed, "because Osborne told her not to and because she had no reason to believe that Edward was not already dead."

"Bloody hell!"

The epithet, very eloquently though very softly spoken, contained more raw anguish than Longworth had ever heard. He glanced at his friend in alarm. "Didn't you know?"

Marwood shook his head. "I had no idea. I would hardly have accused Charlotte of the things I did if I had."

"What exactly did you accuse her of?" Longworth enquired, almost afraid to hear.

"Of being involved with another man behind my back."

"You mean you thought that Charlotte and Edward were—"

"In love?" Marwood finished for him angrily. "Yes, that's exactly what I thought."

"Bloody hell!" Longworth echoed as he began to grasp the full measure of what had happened. "But why

didn't Charlotte tell you the truth about Edward? I can
understand why she would not have told you before his
return, but once Edward was safely back in England,
there would have been no reason for her to have kept
silent. I thought she would have been falling all over
herself to tell you."

"She was, but I never gave her a chance." Briefly,
Marwood went on to explain what had happened.
"Charlotte never even knew I saw them that day in the
garden," he finished woodenly.

"And obviously, at some point along the way you
told her what you thought you had seen."

"In no uncertain terms," Marwood admitted,
recalling all too clearly the look on Charlotte's face
when he had told her exactly what he had thought of
her. Recalling the horror in her eyes—the look of disbelief and betrayal when she had realized that he did not
trust her. "Not only that," Marwood continued
bleakly, "but I told Charlotte that if she did not end the
mockery I thought our betrothal had become, I would."

"You told her that?" Longworth echoed in disbelief.

"That and a few other things." Marwood drew a
ragged breath and then swore heartily. "God, that I had
the power to retract those bloody words now."

"Yes, well, there's not much you can do about that,
I'm afraid," Longworth muttered. He raked his fingers through his own chestnut brown curls. "I wish I
had known why Charlotte's name sounded so familiar
to me that first time you mentioned it. I would have
been able to spare you all this. Unfortunately, it wasn't
until I met up with Kingsley in France and we were
crossing the Channel that he told me who he really was.
That was when I realized why the name was familiar."

Marwood glanced up. "You knew Charlotte's brother?"

Longworth shook his head. "I knew of him. Kingsley was one of Osborne's top men. There wasn't anything the man could not do. No assignment was too dangerous, no code was too difficult to decipher. He's cracked more codes that the rest of us put together."

"If he was so well respected, why didn't you recognize his name right off?" Marwood's tone was unintentionally sharp. "And why had I not heard of him?"

"I wondered about that myself, until I realized that Edward was already working under cover by the time we appeared on the scene. I might have heard his name once in passing during my first few days—long enough to stay in my mind, but not enough to remember where it came from. Kingsley told me that shortly after he joined the department, Osborne started giving him false identities. It seems that he had become something of a target for French espionage. In order to protect him, Osborne was obliged to keep changing his identity. Kingsley never travelled with the same alias twice. Eventually, he began using the code name Robin only."

"But how could a man like that be missing for eight months?" Marwood demanded. "And why wasn't every man in the department out looking for him?"

"Apparently a lot of men were, and most of them were killed in the process," Longworth replied. "Osborne knew the kind of information Kingsley was carrying in his head. When he vanished, the department made every effort to get him back. Unfortunately, the French got wind of it and started their own search. That's when things started to turn nasty. Osborne was forced to pull back when it began to look as though Kingsley had gone into hiding. He simply couldn't afford to lose any more men. So, two months after Kingsley vanished, the gates slammed shut. That's why everything was so hushed up. Osborne asked Charlotte not to mention her brother's disappearance to people who knew of his existence, and to say nothing about having a brother to people who did not. Unfortunately, he had no way of knowing that *you* would eventually become romantically involved with her.''

''And Charlotte, not being aware of my own association with Osborne, would have no reason to tell me about her brother's involvement,'' Marwood said quietly. ''Now it's all falling into place. The letter, the affection I saw between them, Charlotte's astonishment. No wonder she hates me.''

Longworth observed the stricken face of his friend, and shook his head sadly. ''She doesn't hate you, Devon, of that I am quite sure. Remember, I was there. I saw her.''

''She may not hate me, but I'll wager she's not likely to forgive me, either. When I think what I said to her, Nicholas. What I accused her of—''

Marwood broke off, too distressed for words. What an ignorant fool he had been. His own jealousy and lack of faith had cost him the most precious thing in his life, and he had no way of knowing if he would ever be able to get it back. How did one go about regaining someone's trust, Marwood asked himself bleakly. How did one wipe out so grievous a wound as the one he had dealt Charlotte?

''You could try telling her that you love her,'' Longworth said quietly.

Marwood raised his head, unaware that he had uttered the question aloud. But even as he heard Longworth's answer, he shook his head. ''She would probably just throw it back in my face. What good is a love that doubts at the very first opportunity? Hardly a love worth salvaging," he said bitterly.

"Is that how you feel about it?" Longworth asked quietly.

"Of course not!" Marwood blazed. "Charlotte *is* the most important thing in my life. She is my life."

"Then tell her that!" Longworth urged. "Make her see how much you love her. Grovel if you have to, but get her back."

Marwood nodded. He knew that Longworth was right. If it took the rest of his life, he would fight to win back her love.

But having said that, how did he know that winning back Charlotte's love automatically meant reestablishing the bond of trust that went with it? Could that be resurrected as easily?

"Nicholas," Marwood said, his eyes narrowing. "You've been in Town a few days now. What's the latest gossip circulating?"

"Nothing about you and Charlotte, if that's what you're asking," Longworth said. "Though there have been some questions raised about your sudden flight to the country. It would seem, my friend, that you are more conspicuous by your absence than by your presence."

Marwood grunted. "Rumours regarding my whereabouts are the least of my concern. With your help, I can quickly dispatch those. No, it's Charlotte I am worried about. Has news of our broken betrothal leaked out?"

Longworth shook his head. "Not that I've heard. My guess is that Charlotte is keeping it to herself for the moment. A lot has happened to her in the past little while, Devon. Her brother finally coming back, the fight between the two of you. No doubt she is feeling overwhelmed by it all.'' Longworth suddenly remembered Charlotte's parting remark the morning he had gone to see her. ''I don't think she has even told Edward.''

Marwood looked up, a glimmer of hope on his face. ''If she hasn't, there may still be a chance. If I can get to Charlotte and apologize before word leaks out, I may be able to circumvent the whole thing falling apart. There would be questions enough if it did.''

Marwood gave a harsh laugh. ''I still cannot believe it. Edward Kingsley—the Robin—Charlotte's brother. Thank goodness you told me when you did.''

''You would have found out soon enough,'' Longworth said in a matter-of-fact voice. ''News of Kingsley's return is already spreading, and people are hailing the man a hero.''

''At least Charlotte can gain a measure of comfort from that,'' Marwood commented ruefully. ''Nevertheless, I am glad I heard it from you, rather than one of those insufferable Society matrons. Can you imagine the reaction if they were to learn that I was not aware of the identity of the gentleman living in Charlotte's house? By that time, it certainly would have been too late to do anything. But if what you say is true, I may still have time, and knowing that, I intend to do everything in my power to win back Charlotte's trust. God help me, I *have* to win it back!''

TWO NIGHTS LATER, Marwood stood in front of the cheval glass and swore as his normally adept fingers fought with the intricacies of his cravat, causing his valet to sigh as yet another spoiled neckcloth was hurled

onto the floor. But then, it was hardly surprising that
Marwood was in a temper. He didn't like musicales, and
he liked Lady Roxton even less. She was an inquisitive,
interfering woman who spent more time meddling in the
affairs of others than she did in attending to her own,
and under any other circumstances, Marwood would
have gone out of his way to avoid her party.

But these were not any other circumstances, Marwood reminded himself glumly. He was all too aware of
the risks involved in Charlotte's attending Society
functions on her own. People would begin to ask questions, and Charlotte would feel compelled to answer
them with words he would just as soon no one heard.
He had to get to Charlotte and straighten this out. He
had to beg her to forgive him. Doing that far out-
weighed the slight inconvenience of having to socialize
with people he did not particularly like.

Finally, when it seemed that no one short of Mr
Brummell himself would be able to effect a better knot,
Marwood nodded his grudging satisfaction. "It will do,
I suppose," he muttered, glancing at the perfectly tied
Mathematical with a critical eye. "Do I look the part,
Jenkins?"

"Indeed, my lord. Very much, if I may say so."

"Good. I would not want to disappoint Lady Rox
ton, would I?"

If the truth were known, Marwood did not care a fig
whether he disappointed his hostess. All he cared about
was Charlotte, and for her he would put up with pur
gatory!

By the time Marwood arrived at Lady Roxton's
house, the musicale was already under way. He had
purposely arrived late so as not to give Charlotte time
for flight. He left his coat, gloves and hat with the but

ler and then crossed the black-and-white tiled entrance
hall to the music room. The doors to the room were
closed, but beyond it, Marwood could hear the tin-
kling of the harpsichord and a woman singing an old
English ballad. He waited until he heard the sound of
applause, and Lady Roxton's announcement of the next
performer, before pushing open the doors and walking
in.

Several heads turned at the sound of the late arrival,
and several more followed when they heard the gasps of
the first. Lord Marwood's sudden removal from Town
had met with great speculation, but the fact that he was
back—and that his fiancée did not seem to know,
judging by the quickly suppressed look of surprise on
her face—made for the possibility of some extremely
diverting gossip.

Marwood ignored the whispers as he advanced into
the room. By now, such things had ceased to trouble
him. He had not told anyone other than Longworth
that he planned to attend this evening for fear that
Charlotte herself might not attend. Lady Roxton, who,
for her own part, had fully expected the elusive Lord
Marwood to avoid yet another of her assemblies, allowed a smile of pure triumph to curve her lips and
glanced round the room to ensure that everyone knew
of her success.

"Lord Marwood, how delightful to see you!" she
exclaimed, bearing down on him like a battleship in full
sail. "I had feared that perhaps you were going to deprive us of the pleasure of your company yet again."

"Pray forgive my late arrival, Lady Roxton," Marwood murmured. He bowed over the lady's heavily
ringed hand. "I was unavoidably detained."

Lady Roxton, amazed that he had arrived at all, waved away his apologies with the most casual of gestures. "My dear Lord Marwood, pray do not trouble yourself with apologies. The thing is that you are here. Now, do come and have a seat. I fear there is nothing vacant next to your charming fiancée but there does just happen to be a seat here by me."

Marwood nodded and followed his hostess to the seat she indicated. He had not missed her reference to Charlotte as his fiancée and silently sent a prayer of thanks heavenward. Longworth had been right. Charlotte had not yet put about that their betrothal was at an end. So much the better.

As he passed by the row in which she sat, Marwood offered Charlotte a quick smile. She was pale, he noted, but composed. And as beautiful as ever in the gown of off-white silk trimmed with delicate Alençon lace. She noted his regard and inclined her head politely before turning away to address a remark to Laura on her right. It was hardly an endearing look, but at least she had not given him the cut directly, Marwood reflected ruefully.

Taking his seat, Marwood prepared to bide his time until an intermission was announced, when his attention was distracted by the sound of a voice he would just as soon have forgotten.

"Why, good evening, Lord Marwood," the husky feminine voice said close to his ear. "To what do we owe the honour of your presence this evening? Not that I am complaining, of course."

The honey-sweet tones could only belong to one woman, and Marwood forced a stiff smile to his lips. "Good evening, Lady Howard," he replied in what he considered to be a tone of reasonable civility.

Celia, Lady Howard, was as beautiful and alluring as he remembered. In a daring gown of gossamer fine silk, her blond hair framing an elfin face with bewitching green eyes and lush, inviting lips, she was as desirable as a siren. But many a sailor had met his untimely death hearing the siren's song, and Marwood had no intention of casting his own ship upon those rocks. He had already risked destruction once, having enjoyed a brief and tempestuous encounter with her before meeting Charlotte. Once having done so, however, Devon had quickly—far too quickly for Celia's liking—terminated the affair.

"I was not aware that you had returned to Town, my lord," Celia whispered in a low voice. "I have been longing for your return."

Marwood nodded politely, determined not to entangle himself again. "I am but recently returned and have found myself with little time to do anything," he replied, adding pointedly, "and how is Lord Howard this evening?"

The blatant hint caused Celia not the slightest twinge of guilt. "Too well, I am afraid, my lord," she replied, laughing throatily, "but, as you can see, he is not in attendance, which makes my enjoyment of the evening that much more complete. Would you not agree?"

Marwood's smile twisted sardonically. As the bored wife of a very wealthy but considerably older man, Celia, Marwood knew, had not been happy with his rejection. He also knew that not even the announcement of his recent betrothal had been enough to dampen her ardour. Celia could be a very determined woman when she wanted to be. "If you say that his absence improves your enjoyment of the evening, far be it from me

to disagree, Lady Howard. I hope that you will give him
my regards when you return home.''

Celia pouted. ''But how formal you have become,
Devon. You know that I should rather you give *me* your
regard.'' She gave him a provocative look which only a
blind man could have misunderstood. ''You will come
to see me again, won't you, Devon?''

Lord Marwood's dark eyes narrowed. ''I am afraid
not, Lady Howard. I am engaged to be married, and
very content to be so.''

''Really?'' Celia taunted him, clearly disappointed.
''Then why does your dear little fiancée not look as
pleased as you with the prospect, I wonder.''

Celia turned away, a petulant droop to her lower lip.
Her words, however, gave Marwood reason for concern. It would not be long before Charlotte's obvious air
of restraint when in his company was observed. It had
gone unremarked until now because they had not been
seen together since their quarrel. But now that he was
back in London, the sooner his plan was under way, the
better.

''Ladies and gentlemen, if I may have your atten-
tion,'' Lady Roxton said, clapping her hands. ''We shall
continue our evening with a delightful rendition of
'Greensleeves' by Miss Henrietta Glascombe. Miss
Glascombe is accompanied on the harpsichord by Mr.
Edmond Geraldton. Miss Glascombe?''

A polite smattering of applause broke out, and Marwood thankfully turned his attention to the front of the
room. He deliberately fixed his regard on the plain and
woefully shy girl who had taken her position beside the
instrument.

On the other side of the room, Charlotte did the
same. She said something amusing to Laura and then

turned overly bright eyes towards the harpsichord, looking for all the world as though there were nothing in the world she would rather do than listen to Miss Glascombe's halting rendition of the well-loved English folk-song.

But if the truth were known, Charlotte's composure was badly shaken and as far as the entertainment went, she could not have cared whether the Regent himself were standing by the harpsichord waiting to sing. Her enjoyment of the evening had evaporated the moment Lord Marwood set foot in the room.

"Laura, I am feeling a trifle warm all of a sudden," Charlotte said abruptly. "Would you be so good as to accompany me upstairs for a moment?"

Charlotte hated the quaver in her voice but knew there was nothing she could do about it. It was becoming painfully clear to her that she could not be in Devon's presence for more than a few minutes without losing her composure.

"Why, yes of course," Laura replied without hesitation.

Once upstairs in the privacy of the ladies' withdrawing-room, Charlotte sank down onto the chaise and closed her eyes. Her heightened colour had gradually diminished until her face was left looking dreadfully pale.

"Charlotte, are you all right?" Laura asked, clearly concerned by her friend's alarming pallor. "You do not look at all well."

Charlotte opened her eyes and shook her head, trying to ignore the dancing rainbow of lights the movement induced. "I am fine, Laura. Truly. I have just had a lot on my mind lately."

"Well, yes, of course you have," Laura murmured sympathetically. "What with the excitement of your engagement to Lord Marwood, and then your brother's return, and now all the planning for the wedding—"

"Laura, there isn't going to be any wedding," Charlotte replied, forcing herself to say the words aloud. "I have . . . broken off my betrothal to Lord Marwood."

CHAPTER SEVEN

LAURA LOOKED at her friend as though she had suddenly sprouted two heads. "You have done what?"

"It's over. I have broken off my engagement."

"Broken your—but I thought you said—"

"Yes, I know what I said, and I know what you thought. But I was not being completely honest with you when I said that everything was fine between Lord Marwood and myself. In fact, we had a horrible fight."

"Oh, Charlotte, why did you not tell me?"

"Because to be quite truthful, I did not want the news to get about. You know how people like to talk, Laura. There would have been endless speculation as to the reasons why the marriage had been called off."

"Is that why Lord Marwood went away to the country?" Laura enquired delicately.

At Charlotte's nod, Laura sighed and sank down onto the seat next to her. "Oh, dear," she said breathlessly.

"Yes, oh, dear is right," Charlotte agreed. "And you are the only one who knows, apart from Aunt Kittie and Lord Longworth, and I have asked them both to say nothing for the moment. I have not even told Edward yet. I will not have a damper put on his return by making this public knowledge right now. You understand, don't you?"

"Well, yes, I suppose I do," Laura said, looking somewhat dubious in spite of her assertion to the contrary. "But, oh, Charlotte, I am so very sorry. What happened?"

Charlotte shook her head, her eyes darkening with pain as she recalled the bitterness in Devon's voice when he had hurled his accusations at her. "It is of little consequence now. All that matters is that it is over."

After a few more minutes, Charlotte decided that her composure was as much restored as it was likely to be and followed Laura back down the stairs. She quietly slipped into her seat in the music room, her face giving no evidence of the strain she had been under prior to her departure. She was once again the smiling and serene Miss Kingsley. She refused to give anyone the satisfaction of seeing one trace of emotion on her face. If Devon could be cool and calm in the face of Society's scrutiny, so could she!

When Mr. Geraldton's laboured playing, along with Henrietta's thin, falsetto singing finally came to an end, there was more polite applause, though whether it was out of relief or commendation, Charlotte was not sure. Sensing her guests' restlessness, Lady Roxton decided to declare an intermission. "Ladies and gentlemen, refreshments are being served in the main dining-room," she announced brightly. "Shall we adjourn?"

Charlotte rose along with the rest and made her way outside with Laura. Unfortunately, Laura, now having been made aware of the broken betrothal, seemed more disposed towards commenting on Lord Marwood's unexpected appearance than upon the calibre of the entertainments provided.

"I cannot believe he actually came," said Laura, glancing covertly towards the earl.

"And I cannot think why you would find his appearance in any way out of the ordinary," Charlotte admonished. "Lord Marwood was invited the same as we were."

"Yes, but given what has happened—"

"No one here but you and I are aware of what has happened, Laura, and I would caution you to remember that," Charlotte said in a carefully hushed voice. "There will be time enough to make the world aware that Lord Marwood and I are no longer affianced after Edward has been given his hero's welcome. Besides, our quarrel has nothing to do with whether Lord Marwood appears in public or not. He does so frequently, and no doubt will continue to do so. As shall I," Charlotte professed valiantly.

Laura glanced at her friend sympathetically. "Is it too unbearable for you to see him?"

"Unbearable? No," Charlotte admitted slowly. "I admit his... arrival here tonight did catch me somewhat off guard, but it was a momentary lapse and one which I will take pains not to repeat. For the moment, it is imperative that everything appear just as it should be between us."

"I fear you are about to be given opportunity to prove that," Laura whispered, as Marwood approached and drew to a halt in front of them.

"Good evening, Miss Beaufort," Marwood said, before turning to gaze at Charlotte with far more warmth than she expected. "Charlotte. I trust I am not interrupting."

Charlotte maintained her composure admirably. "Not at all, Lord Marwood. Miss Beaufort and I were just commenting on the... quality of the entertainments provided this evening."

"Or their lack thereof," Marwood commented drily. "I would venture to say it has not been one of Lady Roxton's more memorable evenings. Still, I am relieved to hear that it is the rather lacklustre performance of Lady Roxton's guests which has invoked your criticism, Charlotte, rather than my own unexpected appearance," Marwood said in a surprisingly gentle voice.

Charlotte glanced up at him curiously. "On the contrary, my lord, I would say nothing of you, either behind your back or to your face, if it could not be kind."

Lord Marwood chuckled. "Then I can only conclude, my dear, that at times you are left with precious little to say about me at all!"

Charlotte glanced up at Devon, astonished by the bantering familiarity in his tone. They might still have been betrothed from the way he addressed her. By now, others were becoming aware of them conversing, as well as of the heightened colour in Charlotte's cheeks. Lady Roxton, not wishing to miss the opportunity of discovering anything even remotely interesting occurring between the two, quickly made her way to Lord Marwood's side. "And how is everyone here?" she enquired, glancing from one to the other with an expression of benign curiosity.

"Very well, thank you, Lady Roxton," Lord Marwood replied with equanimity. "We were just discussing the merits of honest speech."

"Honest speech? Oh, dear, I try to avoid it wherever possible." Lady Roxton laughed, feigning dismay. "I have found that nothing good ever comes of speaking honestly, especially to one's friends. The last thing they want to hear is what you really think of them."

Marwood nodded in agreement. "My fiancée and I were just commenting on that very fact."

Lady Roxton continued to prattle on, but Charlotte did not hear a word of it. She had turned towards Marwood, disbelief written on her face.

His fiancée? Was he mad? What could possibly have possessed him to say that they were still betrothed? Charlotte quickly opened her fan and plied it to her burning cheeks, looking everywhere but at him. Beside her, Marwood bowed politely. "Will you excuse me, ladies?"

As Marwood moved off, Lady Roxton tapped her fan against her chin in an envious manner. "Such a handsome man, and so obviously devoted to you, Charlotte. You are indeed a very lucky girl. Though, I must say, I did notice a certain... tension about Lord Marwood earlier," Lady Roxton probed gently. "Did you notice that, my dear?"

Charlotte closed her fan with a practised flick of her wrist. "Not at all, Lady Roxton," she lied smoothly. "Lord Marwood is as he ever was."

Lady Roxton smiled, but Charlotte did not miss the quickly suppressed flicker of disappointment in her eyes. "Well, yes, no doubt you are right," Lady Roxton said grudgingly. "Probably nothing more than a case of pre-wedding jitters. Ah, young love," she sighed, more for the benefit of her guests than as a result of any longings of her own. "Speaking of young love, where is your handsome brother this evening? I had hoped that he would honour our little gathering with his presence."

"Unfortunately, Edward was otherwise engaged this evening, Lady Roxton," Charlotte replied, aware that she was fast becoming a very convincing liar. "He did wish me to express his most sincere regrets at having to miss your gathering.''

"What a pity. There are many here who were looking forward to meeting him. Still, there will be other opportunities, I am sure," Lady Roxton was forced to concede.

Standing in a corner nearby, Marwood helped himself to a glass of champagne from the tray of a passing footman, and glanced back towards Charlotte, marvelling at her poise. He had not missed the look of shock on her face when he had called her his fiancée, and had purposely moved away to allow her time to gather herself. But while it was clear that outwardly Charlotte had regained her equilibrium, he knew that she was far from happy. He did not need to see the lingering shadow about her eyes or the faint tremor in her bottom lip when she smiled to know that she was still very confused about what had happened.

"Evening, Marwood.''

"Longworth. Enjoying the evening?''

"Mildly. You?''

"Not as bad as some.''

Longworth nodded, and glanced in Charlotte's direction candidly. "How proceeds the reconciliation?''

"Slowly, I am afraid, but not without hope,'' Marwood replied. "Charlotte did not faint dead away when I referred to her as my fiancée in front of Lady Roxton just now. Have you had any success on your end?''

"Indeed,'' Longworth replied promptly. "I have, in fact, thoroughly quashed any rumours circulating of a rift between the two of you and have put it about that your sudden removal from London was due to pressing matters concerning the management of Marwood Hall.''

Marwood nodded in satisfaction. "Good. If we can at least subdue the rumours until I have had an opportunity to speak with Charlotte, I may be able to stop them from arising at all."

"When do you plan to speak to her?"

"Just as soon as I can get her alone." Marwood's eyes were shuttered. "I cannot afford to lose any more time than I already have."

Across the crowded room, Charlotte pretended to listen to the conversation going on around her and carefully stifled a yawn. Her feet were aching, she had a splitting headache and she wanted nothing more than to leave. She was tired of having to pretend that everything was all right. Nothing at all was right. She wanted to go home to be alone with her misery and her anger.

Yes, her anger, Charlotte told herself with as much defiance as she could muster. How dared Devon presume upon her like that, pretending that they were still betrothed. He'd had no right. In fact, she had no idea why he would want to. After all, he had already made his feelings on the subject perfectly clear, hadn't he?

"How are you feeling, Charlotte?" Laura asked, reappearing at her side.

Grateful for the distraction, Charlotte smiled. "A little tired. I own I will be relieved when this evening is over."

Laura gazed down at the tip of her pale pink slippers and sighed. "Yes, I am sure it must be very difficult for you. It is good of Lord Marwood to go along with your plan not to tell people of the betrothal, though. You certainly would not know by his tone of voice that there was anything wrong. And that reference to your being his fiancée in front of Lady Roxton was entirely convincing. Especially as she was looking to find fault."

"But that is just what I do not understand, Laura," Charlotte replied in frustration. "Lord Marwood and I did not come to any kind of... agreement. His reference to me as his fiancée earlier came as a complete shock! The last time I saw him, he told me in no uncertain terms exactly what he thought of me and that if I did not break off the betrothal, he would! We certainly did not come to any agreement."

"But are you sure you did not misunderstand him, Charlotte?" Laura asked hopefully. "Lord Marwood has been anything but short with you tonight."

"I understood him perfectly well," Charlotte replied, unable to forget the nature of their quarrel. "Our betrothal is well and truly over, Laura. But I have absolutely no idea why Lord Marwood is pretending that it is not!"

THE FOLLOWING MORNING, Charlotte sat on the settee in the yellow salon and listlessly threaded her needle. Her eyes focused beyond the square of fabric in her tambour to a face which had no right to be there. Devon's behaviour last night had been totally inexplicable, as well as irrational, and Charlotte was not sure which she had found more distressing—that he had treated her with such warmth and consideration, or that he had been presumptuous enough to do so!

"Wool-gathering again, Lotte?" Edward asked, breaking into her thoughts.

Charlotte jumped and felt the colour surge into her cheeks. "Edward, you really must learn to make some sound when you come into a room," she scolded him fiercely. "You give a soul palpitations!"

Edward glanced down at her face with an look of contrition in his brilliant blue eyes. "Sorry, Lotte, but

I'm afraid stealth has become second nature to me now.
I doubt I could make a lot of noise even if I tried."

"Well, try anyway." Charlotte's smile removed the
sting from her words, and she paused for a moment to
admire his appearance. What a difference a few weeks
had made. The hollows in his cheeks were filling out,
and his clothes no longer made him look like an ill-
dressed scarecrow. Indeed, he looked as fine as five-
pence this morning in a smart new jacket over a pair of
smooth-fitting breeches, his legs encased in Hessians so
highly polished that she could see her face in them.

"My, Edward, how splendid you look," Charlotte
complimented him. "I daresay the ladies will swoon at
the very sight of you."

"Thank you, Lotte," he said, sketching her a little
bow. "And speaking of ladies, I have been meaning to
take you to task over that little trick you played on poor
Miss Beaufort. Another errand, indeed."

"Oh, now, Edward, don't scold. I could see that you
were just looking for an excuse to be with Laura, and I
thought it was very good of me to provide you with an
opportunity so quickly. I know how shy you are with
the ladies."

"Do you, indeed?" he responded, grinning. "And
since when did you decide to take it upon yourself to
arrange my love life for me?"

"From the moment I saw you and Laura looking at
each other with calf's eyes," Charlotte informed him.
"Good heavens, Teddy, I could practically feel the vi-
brations in the air."

"Yes, well, the next time you are inclined to feel vi-
brations, do me a favour and ignore them," Edward
replied, trying to hide his laughter. "You had poor Miss
Beaufort nearly beside herself with embarrassment.

Great-aunt Gertrude indeed. Took me almost an hour to settle the poor girl down."

Charlotte's mouth twitched "I would not have thought an hour in your company would settle any girl down, Teddy. More likely it would unsettle her for a week. Especially now that you are quite the hero," Charlotte pointed out proudly.

Some of the sparkle faded from Edward's eyes. "What nonsense," he muttered darkly. "I wish to God everyone would forget all about it. There was nothing heroic about what went on, I can assure you. Still, I did not come down here to dampen your spirits. Came to ask you if you'd care to join me for a drive."

Charlotte brightened momentarily. "A drive?"

"Yes. I thought I would take you and Miss Beaufort to the fair. Miss Beaufort told me that the two of you rather enjoyed yourselves last year. She informed me that you even slipped away and had your fortune told by the old Gypsy, though she was most annoyed when you would not tell her about it."

At the mention of the Gypsy, Charlotte's own smile abruptly faded. She had never spoken to anyone of what the woman had said. "It is good of you to ask, Teddy, but no, thank you. I think perhaps I should stay home." She indicated the embroidery in her lap. "I have been quite remiss of late in attending to things domestic."

"Have you, indeed?" Edward frowned, aware that as soon as they had stopped joking, Charlotte had slipped back into the mood which seemed to have taken hold of her since shortly after his return. "I wonder. You have not been looking too happy, Lotte, and that's not like you. Especially now, when you have so much to be happy about."

Painfully aware that she had little other than her brother's return to be happy about, Charlotte shook her head. She hoped her smile was convincing as she uttered the bald-faced lie. "I am fine, Teddy. Really. And I am delighted to hear that you are taking Laura to the fair. Apart from the fact that she did have a good time last year, she will enjoy seeing it all the more with you."

Edward heard the assurances, saw the smile and didn't believe a word. "Lotte, are you sure you're feeling quite the thing?"

"Of course, Edward. Why would you ask?"

"No reason," he replied, adding with a casual shrug, "I just thought that you were looking a touch more tired than usual." He grinned boyishly. "Perhaps you should have Aunt Kittie mix up one of her tonics."

"Heavens, anything but that! Now go and have a good time. And stop worrying about me."

Edward bent down and pressed a quick kiss against her dark hair. "I shall be home in time for dinner."

In the silence following Edward's departure, Charlotte let the embroidery slip to her lap, well aware that her brother was right. She had not been sleeping well. Her dreams, like most of her waking moments, were filled with thoughts of Devon, until she had long since ceased to hope that sleep would offer her the escape she so desperately sought.

Unexpectedly, the words of the Gypsy's prophecy came back to her. The old woman had been right, Charlotte admitted. Devon had brought her joy and pain.

By love's hand shall you be condemned. She had been right about that, too. Edward's letter—the very one she had waited so long to receive—had been the one which had ultimately destroyed her relationship with Devon. What then, of the last part of the prophecy?

"Good afternoon, Charlotte."

Charlotte spun round on the love seat. "Devon! What are you doing here?" Her eyes went beyond him to the door. "How did you get in?"

Marwood slowly made his way to her side. "I bribed Dickens," he admitted with a lopsided grin. "I hope I am not intruding."

Charlotte lifted her chin, praying that he could not see how furiously her heart was beating. "You are, and I hope you will not be offended if I ask you to leave."

"May I not speak with you a moment, Charlotte?"

"I cannot imagine what you would have to say to me, my lord." Charlotte willed her voice not to tremble. "I thought you had already made your feelings painfully clear."

"I made my feelings clear before I realized the truth of the matter. That is what I would speak to you about. About . . . Edward."

Charlotte gazed up at the man standing quietly beside her, torn by the disturbing pull of her emotions. "Very well, my lord. Since you have gone to the trouble of bribing your way in here, I suppose you may as well say what you have come to."

Marwood heard the stiffness in her voice. "Will you not make this easy for me, Charlotte?"

"I see no reason why I should, my lord. You did not make it easy for me that day in the Park."

"No, I did not," Marwood admitted. "And I have not stopped regretting it for a moment since I discovered my folly."

The softness in his voice tugged painfully at her heart. Charlotte's gaze was shuttered as it rested on his face.

"How did you come to discover your folly, my lord, since you obviously did not hear it from me?"

"Lord Longworth informed me of it upon his return to London."

"Lord Longworth?" Charlotte's composure slipped. "Lord Longworth knew of this? But how?"

"Were you not aware that it was Longworth who brought your brother out of France?"

"Dear God!" Charlotte paled. "No, I was not. Why did he not tell me? Or Edward? They were both here that morning." She gazed at him in silent appeal. "Why did one of them not tell me?"

"No doubt they had their reasons," Marwood said, knowing very well why no mention had been made of the fact.

"Oh, bother men and their stubborn pride!" Charlotte said with uncharacteristic vehemence. "If they had but told me—I owe Lord Longworth so much. He must think me terribly ill-mannered for not having said anything."

"Your thanks are not necessary, Charlotte," Marwood replied, though not unkindly. "Longworth did what he did for his country, not for you."

"Nevertheless, it was my brother he brought home, Lord Marwood, not some *stranger* as you were inclined to think at the time."

Marwood felt the sting behind her words. "Charlotte, I can only apologize for believing you guilty of such a thing. I was jealous, can you not understand that? Can you not see that I was blinded, first by the letter, and then by the sight of you in another man's arms? What was I to think?"

"You should have thought that I would not have betrayed you, my lord, no matter what you saw," Charlotte replied in a tight little voice. "Things are not always what they seem."

"No, I am very well aware of that." He looked down at her face regretfully. "Will you not forgive me then, Charlotte? Is there no room in your heart for me?"

Charlotte momentarily closed her eyes against the sight of that face—the face of a man who had caused her more pain than anyone had a right to. "You did not trust me, my lord," she whispered tremulously, "and that I cannot easily forgive. Nor can I forgive your behaviour last evening at Lady Roxton's. I have no idea why you would wish to perpetrate this . . . charade."

"Charade?" he repeated.

"Yes. With regard to our betrothal." Charlotte turned her back to him as she uttered the words. "We both know that our engagement is at an end, yet you seem strangely reluctant to let it be known."

Marwood gazed at her thoughtfully. "No more reluctant than you, I wouldn't have thought."

She whirled back round. "I?"

"It was you who first chose to say nothing, Charlotte. When I returned to London, I fully expected to hear people discussing our . . . *mésentente*. I think you can understand my surprise when I learned that no one, in fact, seemed to know that we had . . . changed our minds."

Charlotte lifted her chin defiantly. "I had my reasons for keeping my silence, Lord Marwood. My brother had only recently returned to England, and I did not wish the news of his homecoming to be dampened by our own decidedly less happy news. Nor did I wish Edward to be unduly concerned about me. He has had a bad enough time of it over the past three years."

"I give you no argument over that," Marwood said. He walked across to the leaded window and gazed out, not even pretending an interest in the activities he saw in the street below. "So, Charlotte, where would you have us go from here?"

"My lord?"

"Well, since you flatly refuse to accept my apology and have informed me in no uncertain terms that you have no intention of changing your mind, I should like to know how you would like to proceed." He turned and glanced at her, noting the confusion in her eyes. "It seems that nothing is to be gained by prolonging it now. I only perpetrated the charade, as you call it, in order to gain time to talk to you. But now that I have, and have gained nothing by it, I suppose I must ask you how you wish to go on? Would you like me to circulate the news that our betrothal is at an end, or do you wish to do so yourself?"

Faced with the question, Charlotte suddenly found herself at a loss for words. What did she really want? Did she truly wish people to know that it was over between herself and the Earl of Marwood? Did she want to acknowledge it herself?

Drawing a deep breath, Charlotte began to reply when the sound of a commotion directly overhead startled her into silence. She heard the sound of glass shattering, followed by a muffled cry and then a heavy thump.

Marwood's eyes shot upwards. "What the hell was that?"

Charlotte was already moving towards the door. "I don't know. Aunt Kittie's room is directly above this one."

When they got to the top of the stairs, Anna was standing in the hallway outside Aunt Kittie's room, wringing her hands. "Oh, Miss Charlotte, she isn't answering! I didn't know what to do."

"Hush, Anna." Charlotte brushed past the girl and opened her aunt's door, stopping on the threshold in horror. She did not need to ask what had happened. The sight of the overturned chair, the shattered remains of the broken medicine bottle and the heavy smell of lavender gave clear testimony to the cause of the accident. The sight of her aunt's crumpled body on the floor beside the wardrobe, a nasty bruise already discolouring the skin around her eye, showed the result. "Aunt Kittie! Oh, Devon—"

He was there before she had a chance to finish, his hands like bands of steel on her arms, supporting her. She could almost feel his strength flowing into her. "Send for Dr. Palfrey," he ordered, "and tell him to get here as fast as he can."

Charlotte nodded. She crossed to the bell-pull and summoned Dickens while Devon gently scooped the unconscious woman up in his arms and laid her upon the bed.

The butler arrived momentarily. "Dickens, send one of the lads for Dr. Palfrey," Charlotte said quickly. "My aunt has had a fall and will require attention as soon as possible."

Glancing towards the bed, Dickens went nearly as white as Charlotte. "I'll go, Miss Charlotte," he said, collecting himself. "I would feel better attending to it myself."

Charlotte nodded, thanking him with her eyes. She turned to the distraught maid. "Anna, go downstairs and ask Mrs. Bramble for some hot water and clean cloths. You and I will clean this up before the doctor arrives."

"Yes, Miss Charlotte," the girl whimpered and scurried off.

Charlotte bit her lip and hurried to her aunt's side. Her heart was beating furiously. "Oh Devon, how very pale she looks."

"She'll be all right," Marwood said, not taking his eyes from her aunt's face. "What the devil was she doing up there, anyway?"

Charlotte sighed. "Trying to get down one of her remedies. I've warned her to be careful, but she *will* put those heavy bottles on top of the wardrobe. I don't know how many times I—oh!" Charlotte caught her breath as her aunt's translucent eyelids fluttered open. "Aunt Kittie?" Charlotte whispered, kneeling down close to her aunt's pallid face.

"Charlotte?"

"I am here, dearest. You are going to be all right. Dr. Palfrey is coming."

"Head . . . hurts," Aunt Kittie said, closing her eyes. Charlotte glanced at Marwood in dismay.

"Talk to her, Charlotte," he ordered softly. "Try to keep her awake."

"Lord . . . Marwood?" Aunt Kittie ventured. "Charlotte, is . . . Lord Marwood . . . here?"

"Yes, Aunt. Devon is here."

To Charlotte's amazement, a tiny smile appeared. "Good. Don't like to see you . . . unhappy." The eyelids fluttered closed again.

"Devon?" Charlotte whispered, clutching the tiny hand in hers, afraid to look away.

"She's still with us, Charlotte," Marwood soothed. "Keep talking to her. Don't let her go to sleep."

Charlotte sat at her aunt's side and talked. She talked of anything and everything that came into her head, nonsense or otherwise, just so long as the sound of her voice kept her aunt awake. Marwood stood by, silently watching. Finally, they heard the crunch of carriage wheels on the gravel below.

Charlotte glanced up quickly. "Is it Dr. Palfrey?"

At the window, Marwood nodded. "Thank God." The relief in his voice was evident.

In minutes, Dr. Palfrey was in the room. He quickly examined the elderly woman, confirming that apart from the nasty bruise forming at her temple and a cut on her shoulder, she had sustained no broken bones.

"She's had a nasty bump, but I don't think it's anything more serious than that. Thankfully, the cut on her shoulder is clean," Dr. Palfrey said when he had finished his examination. "Just see that she rests and try to keep her quiet. At her age, shock can sometimes cause more harm than the actual injury."

"You're sure she is going to be all right?" Charlotte asked.

Dr. Palfrey grinned. "Your aunt may be small, Miss Kingsley, but she has determination enough for two. Helps that she has such a hard head, too!" He took a bottle out of his bag and gave it to Charlotte. "Give her some of this when she wakes up. It will help to ease her pain. And don't let her take any of those blasted remedies of hers."

Charlotte managed a weak smile. "Thank you, Dr. Palfrey."

Marwood shook the doctor's hand. "Thank you for coming so quickly, Hugh. I'll see you out."

Marwood walked the doctor downstairs, leaving Charlotte alone with her aunt.

"Charlotte?"

"I'm here, Aunt Kittie," Charlotte replied softly. "How are you feeling, dearest?"

"I have felt ... better. Am I going to live?"

At that, Charlotte experienced the first urge to laugh he had felt all day. "Yes, you are. Dr. Palfrey told us ou were a tough old bird," she said affectionately.

"Impertinent!" Aunt Kittie grimaced. "I shall ave ... a word with him when I am on my feet again." he opened her eyes and delicately sniffed the air. "Botheration! I was afraid of that."

"Afraid of what?"

"The lavender."

"I beg your pardon?"

"The jar of lavender. It broke, didn't it. I can smell ."

"Never mind the lavender, Aunt Kittie. How many mes have I told you—" Charlotte abruptly bit back he rest of the scolding, remembering what the doctor ad advised. Instead she said, "I want you to rest now, unt. Dr. Palfrey said you are to stay in bed." Charotte tucked the blankets up around her chin. "Are you arm enough?"

"Yes, though perhaps you could have Anna make up poultice of ..."

"I am not going to have Anna make up anything." Charlotte was firm. "Dr. Palfrey was most insistent that ou use the medicine he left."

"But my own are better."

"Aunt Kittie!"

"Oh, very well. But if I have any bruises, I want you fetch my wormwood balm and—"

Charlotte shook her head in resignation. "I think he as right. You do have a hard head!"

"Charlotte?"

"Yes!"

"Lord Marwood was here?"

Charlotte faltered. "Y-yes. He's just seeing the doctor out."

Aunt Kittie smiled. "He is a good man, Charlotte."

"Yes, I know," Charlotte replied after the briefest of hesitations. "Now I want you to rest."

"So happy you and Lord Marwood—"

The rest of the sentence was left unfinished as Aunt Kittie drifted off to sleep. Pressing a tender kiss against the wrinkled cheek, Charlotte quietly rose and turned towards the door.

Marwood was standing in the doorway, watching her.

"She's asleep," Charlotte said lamely.

He nodded. "So I see. She is going to be fine, Charlotte. I think she is more concerned about you than she is about herself right now."

Charlotte blushed. "I take it you heard what she said."

"I heard, but it need not signify," Marwood informed her quietly. "She will recover whether you and I stay together or not. But there will be another time to speak of that. You need to get some rest yourself."

"Yes, I think I do," Charlotte replied. She gazed at the man who stood in front of her, and suddenly felt unutterably weary. "Thank you, Devon. I...don't know what I would have done without you."

"You would have managed, Charlotte," Marwood said. "You are a very strong young lady, and one quite capable of dealing with any situation. Now go to your room and get some rest. I shall see myself out."

"Devon?"

Marwood turned around. "Yes?"

"What we spoke of earlier," Charlotte began awkwardly, "about...our betrothal. Perhaps under the circumstances, we should...wait a little while before we say anything. You heard what the doctor said about...not upsetting Aunt Kittie."

Marwood watched Charlotte in silence for a few minutes, his expression veiled. Then he said, "If it is what you wish."

Charlotte nodded, feeling the tightness back in her throat. "It is."

"Very well. Then that is how it shall be. To all intents and purposes, we are still engaged. Only you and I will know differently. But I think it only fair to tell you, Charlotte," Marwood said, walking towards her until he stood so close that she could smell the disturbingly masculine scent he wore, "that you must be the one to say when this...charade is at an end. When you feel that your aunt is well enough to hear the truth, we shall make it known. Until then, I shall govern myself accordingly. Agreed?"

Charlotte nodded again, unable to put what she was feeling into words.

With a smile that could have meant anything, Marwood bowed, and turned to go, leaving Charlotte in the room with her sleeping aunt, tired and even more confused than she could ever remember having felt!

CHAPTER EIGHT

"TOUCHÉ!" Lord Longworth cried, his voice muffled by the protective mask he wore over his face. "I believe that's my bout, Barrymore. Care to try another?"

The tall, rather inelegant man standing opposite him removed his mask and shook his head. "I think not, Longworth. My dignity has suffered enough for one day."

Longworth laughed. "Now, Fitz, there's no need to sound so dejected. You've not been at this sport long enough to become discouraged by the loss of a few rounds." Longworth glanced at the foil in his hand with respect. "It takes time to master the blade, and 'tis not so easily managed as one might think. Besides," he added, "I owed you this. You gave me a proper send-off at the table the other week. I've not gone home with pockets that empty in a very long while."

"Well, I daresay we all have our talents." Barrymore turned at the sound of a new arrival. "Ah, Marwood. I trust you are in fine spirits this morning."

Marwood, who was in neither fine spirits nor a particularly amiable frame of mind, cast a tolerant glance towards the speaker and nodded more affably towards Longworth. "Given the events of last evening, I am amazed to find myself up yet. I did not reach my bed til nearly three this morning."

"Indeed? And whose bed were you in until three this morning?" Barrymore enquired boldly.

Marwood's dark brows rose fractionally. "Inquisitive, aren't you, Barrymore?"

"Well, I, too, was at Lord Dreighton's last evening, my dear Marwood, and I saw you leave there no later than one. Hence, if you did not reach your own bed for nearly two hours, I can only conclude you were in someone else's for the duration."

Marwood shook his head. "Your jest is in poor taste, Barrymore. As you well know, I am promised to Miss Kingsley."

Barrymore shrugged. "To my knowledge, that has never prevented a fellow from keeping his bed warm at night. And you ain't married yet. I noticed that your intended appeared a trifle cool the last time the two of you were together."

Marwood's countenance darkened ominously. "What my fiancée does is no concern of yours, Barrymore, and I would advise you to watch what you say lest you find yourself at the opposite end of my blade."

Barrymore's mocking grin vanished in a trice. "You don't frighten me, Marwood. If you wish to fight, pick up your weapon and let us take our places on the floor." He brandished his foil in what he believed to be a suitably threatening gesture. "I've half a mind to teach you a lesson here and now!"

"Teach him a lesson? Zounds, Barrymore, you must have half a mind to contemplate such foolishness," Longworth observed in a dry tone. "Marwood would have you skewered before you'd even had time to assume the opening position."

Barrymore blanched. Having forgotten his own lack of expertise in the heat of the moment, he recognized the wisdom of withdrawing the comment. It did not, however, prevent him from casting a rather arrogant glance in the earl's direction. "Sorry, Marwood. Didn't mean any slight. No doubt your little bride-to-be was not feeling quite the thing. Happens to them all, I understand. And I did see you speaking with Lady Howard."

Marwood unwrapped his foil with a marked lack of concern. "Is that supposed to have some significance, Barrymore? I often speak to ladies with whom I am acquainted."

"Rather more than just acquainted, weren't you?" Barrymore's lip curled. "I understand you and Celia were quite . . . close at one time."

Marwood straightened and looked the man directly in the face. "Whatever passed between Lady Howard and myself in the past is exactly that, Barrymore. Past. And I would bring to your attention the fact that I did not open the conversation with Lady Howard the other night."

Barrymore smiled lazily. "Is there a difference as to who initiates conversation?"

"There is to me," Marwood replied tersely. "As I've told you, I am betrothed and I do not intend to give my lady any cause for unhappiness. Either before or after our wedding."

"Perhaps you should direct Barrymore here into the path of Lady Howard," Longworth suggested, seeking to alleviate some of the tension between the two men. "Since Celia is so obviously looking for new diversions."

Marwood allowed himself a brief smile. "I think poor Fitz has already tested the waters and found them a little chilly."

Lord Barrymore flushed and pointedly ignored Marwood. "I am quite capable of finding my own *chère amie*, thank you, Longworth. In fact, I've had my eye on a rather enticing little dancer for the past few weeks now. Saw her at the theatre, and if I don't miss my guess, she is in need of someone to take care of her."

"Then by all means, take care of her, Barrymore," Lord Marwood advised him. "I should hate to think of you spending your evenings alone."

Barrymore shot the earl a suspicious glance, not at all sure that Marwood wasn't enjoying a jest at his expense. He had certainly been known to in the past. His eyes narrowed coldly. "I wonder if you realize how much money has been wagered on your not making it all the way to the altar, old boy." Barrymore fastened his cloak around his shoulders and winked meaningfully. "Odds are stacked against you."

Marwood shrugged off the remark. "As there are those who would bet on whether the rain will fall two days in a row, I don't doubt that there are. However, as I said, those who have wagered against me are destined to be out of pocket. I intend to marry Miss Kingsley."

Barrymore drew himself up. "Then I wish you all the best. Your servant, gentlemen."

"Barrymore."

When the door finally closed behind him, Marwood's smile faded. Beside him, Longworth scowled. "Puffed up popinjay."

"Pay no mind to what he says, Nicholas, the man is a buffoon," Marwood said dismissively. "Always has been."

Longworth rubbed his hand along the blade thoughtfully. "The man may be a buffoon, but he did notice Charlotte's coolness the other night. And you may be assured that if he did, other people did, too. Or am I mistaken and it is no longer an issue?" Longworth glanced at his friend hopefully. "Have things improved between you and Miss Kingsley?"

"No, I fear they have not," Marwood replied regretfully. "But I was damned if I was going to let Barrymore know. He was looking for something to take back to his cronies, and I certainly wasn't about to give it to him."

"No, of course not. Still, it's a pity," Longworth said. "I'd hoped that perhaps you had been able to repair the damage."

"I am beginning to think the damage irreparable." Marwood reached for his foil and absently tested the tip. "I went to see Charlotte yesterday."

"And?"

"And she informed me in no uncertain terms that it was time I put an end to this charade."

"By Jove, that was plain speaking," Longworth said ruefully. "Is it to be circulated, then?"

"No. Unfortunately, though perhaps fortunately for me, Charlotte's aunt suffered a fall while I was there and quite innocently put a halt to the proceedings. The doctor advised Charlotte that it would be better not to upset her aunt in any way for a few days. I believe poor Miss Harper thought my presence in the house meant that Charlotte and I had been able to resolve our differences and she was obviously very pleased. Charlotte asked me not to say anything to the contrary until her aunt was well enough to hear the truth. It seems as close as we are going to get to any kind of compromise."

Longworth's face fell. "Little more than a temporary reprieve, then."

"I fear that is all it is." Marwood picked up his fencing mask. "I believe in my heart that Charlotte still has feelings for me, but I also know that she is quite unable to forgive me for what I accused her of."

"And what are your feelings on the matter?" Longworth asked.

Marwood smiled sadly. "I would marry her tomorrow, but not unless I know that I have her trust. I cannot change her mind, Nicholas, nor can I undo the damage I have done. I fear I must resign myself to the fact that we have reached an impasse."

Longworth studied the face of his friend for a few minutes. Even a blind man could see that Marwood was anything but resigned to the sorry state of his relationship with Charlotte.

"Well, buck up, old friend, these things often have a way of working themselves out," Longworth said in an encouraging tone.

"Yes, oftimes they do, but I am not expecting any miracles here." Marwood pulled the fencing mask down over his face and followed Longworth onto the mat. "I doubt there is any way of showing Charlotte that I am not the untrustworthy cad she thinks I am. Are you ready?"

Longworth took his position. "Indeed. I've a mind to get back at you for that drubbing I took at your hands last week."

Beneath the mask, Marwood grinned. "Do you think yourself ready?"

"I intend to give it my best. *En garde!*"

AT LADY WILTON'S SOIRÉE the following evening, Charlotte, exquisitely attired in a gown of soft lilac silk with matching elbow-length gloves and dainty satin slippers, recounted the story of her aunt's accident to a sympathetic audience of Lady Broughton, Lady Bering and Mrs. Hortense Booker-Smythe.

"Oh, poor Miss Harper," Lady Bering murmured. "How dreadful for her. Thank goodness Lord Marwood was on hand. Otherwise she might have lain there for hours until the doctor arrived."

"Dr. Palfrey assured you there was no damage of a lasting nature?" Lady Broughton asked.

"None, thank goodness. She has a rather nasty cut on her shoulder from the broken glass and a bruise on her temple where she hit the chair, but other than that, she is fine. He left me some medicine for the pain."

"Good man, Palfrey," Hortense said in a strong voice. "Had him round to see Booker-Smythe when he took a fall at Melton. Nasty gash. Fell right onto the blessed fence." She shook her head and tutted. "Terrible rider. Never could take anything at a gallop."

Charlotte tried not to laugh. Hortense Booker-Smythe was a somewhat horse-faced woman who enjoyed riding to hounds and was rumoured to smoke her husband's cheroots. She also had a reputation for speaking her mind in a most forthright manner, and at the most inconvenient of times. "Well, Lady Broughton," she asked now. "What do you think of the rumours circulating about Lady Howard?"

Lady Bering's face lit up. "Rumours? What rumours?"

Beside her, Lady Broughton stiffened. "Hortense, *please!* The woman is standing just over there."

"Well, what of it? Everyone knows that Celia has had more stallions than a brood mare in the field. The fact that she is rumoured to have found a new one shouldn't come as a surprise to anyone."

Lady Bering gasped in shocked delight. "A paramour?"

Hortense nodded. "Course, it wasn't as if the gel was ever in love with her husband," she rattled on, oblivious to Lady Broughton's intimidating stare. "She knew what he was before she married him. Rich as Croesus, but as boring as a judge. No doubt she's looking for a little spark in her life."

"Really, Hortense!" Lady Broughton looked down her nose, utterly appalled. "You almost sound as though you approve of what she is doing. A lady must observe the proprieties, no matter what the state of her marriage. Is that not right, Lady Bering?"

"Hmm? Oh, yes, indeed!" Lady Bering replied, belatedly recalled to the need to say something suitably censorious. "It would be shocking ton for a married lady to openly flaunt her affairs."

"But quite acceptable for her to conduct them discreetly, eh?" Hortense remarked drily.

Charlotte prudently moved away from the group. Hortense Booker-Smythe might be outspoken, but she certainly had an excellent grasp of Society's foibles. It seemed that it was perfectly all right for a man or a woman to take a lover, as long as the niceties were observed. One could bend Society's rules, but never break them. Charlotte was still pondering that when Lord Marwood joined her a short while later.

It was their first appearance in public together since their mutual agreement regarding their engagement, and thus far, things were progressing reasonably well. Marwood, elegantly turned out in formal evening attire, was politely attentive and acting as a fiancé should. He smiled as he responded to the congratulations extended to them and never for a moment gave anyone the impression that he and Charlotte were not the happily betrothed couple they appeared to be.

"Can I get anything for you, Charlotte?" he enquired of her now.

"Thank you, my lord, perhaps later." Charlotte risked a quick glance at his face. His expression was inscrutable, a handsome mask giving nothing away. She sighed softly. "I...appreciate your patience, Lord Marwood. I know this is not easy for you."

Marwood turned to her and shook his head. "It is not easy for either of us, Charlotte, but I daresay it is a good deal better than exposing the truth at this particular moment. There is your aunt's health to consider."

Charlotte nodded. She was well aware how quickly gossip would circulate once anything was said. She had not even had the courage to tell Edward the truth about her relationship with Devon, let alone Aunt Kittie, and they both deserved to hear it from her rather than anyone else.

"Well, if it isn't the happy couple," Barrymore drawled. "I trust the wedding arrangements are well under way?"

Charlotte quickly took up her role again as Lord Barrymore and Lady Howard joined them. "Quite so, thank you, Lord Barrymore."

"I should tell you, Miss Kingsley, that there is a great deal of interest being generated by your nuptials," Barrymore glanced briefly at Marwood. "Don't believe anyone thought the elusive Earl of Marwood would ever be caught in the parson's mousetrap. My compliments to you."

"Yes, indeed, Miss Kingsley." Lady Howard remarked. "You seem to have accomplished the impossible. I did not think there was a net strong enough to hold the dashing Lord Marwood." Celia glanced up at him and pouted provocatively. "I know mine was not."

Charlotte stiffened, aware of Barrymore's hastily muffled laughter. Marwood, however, handled the situation with his usual aplomb. "On the contrary, Lady Howard, Charlotte needs no nets to hold me. The strings of love are infinitely fine, but they are stronger by far than any net." He put one arm possessively around Charlotte's slim waist and guided her away. "Come, my dear. Perhaps you would care for those refreshments now."

Charlotte nodded and rigidly turned away, aware that her cheeks were burning. The memory of Hortense Booker-Smythe's earlier conversation came unpleasantly to mind. "And what exactly did Lady Howard mean by that remark, my lord?" Charlotte enquired when they were out of hearing distance.

"Ignore Celia," Marwood said briefly. "What she says is not worth listening to."

"Perhaps not, but what she said is obviously rooted in truth. Did you have an affair with her?"

Marwood's reply was just as direct. "Would it bother you to learn that I had?"

Charlotte lifted her eyes to his. "I asked you a question, my lord. Will you not give me an answer?"

"Is the answer so very important, given the nature of our subterfuge?" Marwood asked quietly. "We are here to fool the others, Charlotte, not ourselves. A glass of ratafia?"

Charlotte accepted the proffered drink, well aware that she had been put off. But she knew she had her answer. And the fact that it was yes did nothing to lessen her irritation.

When the dancing began, Marwood took Char
lotte's hand and led her out onto the floor for a waltz
Charlotte had always enjoyed dancing with Devon. I
had been a heady feeling, whirling about the floor in th
arms of the man she loved. But now, as she felt th
warmth of Devon's hand on her waist, Charlotte bit he
lip, aware of the heat building under his touch. He wa
so very close, their bodies nearly touching. The musk
scent of his cologne filled her nostrils, tantalizing he
senses. Even now, she could look up into his face an
see the flecks of gold in his eyes, and the dark, curlin
lashes framing them. He had surprisingly long eye
lashes for a man, Charlotte noted absently.

"You look deep in thought, Charlotte," Marwood
said, startling her.

Charlotte slid her gaze away from him. "Not really
my lord. I was merely pondering the inequities of na
ture."

Marwood lifted one eyebrow but made no comment
and they finished the rest of the waltz in silence. When
at the end of it Marwood surrendered Charlotte to he
next partner, he tried to ignore the undeniable stab o
jealousy the sight of her smiling easily at another gen
tleman caused him, all too aware of the stiffness whic
had coloured their own dance. He returned to his plac
by the elaborate Chinese screen and stood watchin
Charlotte in a decidedly ill humour.

"Miss Kingsley is looking particularly fetching thi
evening," Lord Longworth observed, suddenly ap
pearing at Marwood's side. "Any progress?"

Marwood shook his head. "No. Nor had I expecte
any. At times, Charlotte can be a very stubborn lady.'

"Well, I must say you are both doing an excellent jo
of acting the part," Longworth complimented hir

quietly. "No one looking at the two of you would ever guess there was anything amiss."

"Unless they happened to hear us talking." Devon's mouth twisted. "Thanks to that clunch, Barrymore, Charlotte is now suspicious about my past involvement with Celia. She raked me over the coals quite mercilessly."

"I am very glad to hear it."

Marwood glared at him. "I beg your pardon?"

Longworth followed Charlotte's progress around the floor with his eyes. "Think about it, Dev. Charlotte may have broken off your engagement, but if she didn't give a damn about you, she would hardly be upset over your involvement with Celia—past or present—now would she?"

Marwood hesitated, and then slowly began to smile. "Do you know, Nicholas, I think I am finally beginning to understand what Lavinia sees in you."

"Don't know why it's taken you so long to figure it out," Longworth said, giving him a rakish smile. "I always told you I was a sterling fellow. Shall I see you tomorrow morning at O'Shaunessy's?"

"Eleven o'clock, and try not to be late," Marwood said, before dutifully moving off to collect his next partner.

Longworth winked, and likewise turned away. "Wouldn't dream of it, old boy."

Standing quietly behind the Chinese screen, Lady Howard waited until both gentlemen had moved off before cautiously stepping out, a smile of complete and utter satisfaction on her face.

So, all was not well between Lord Marwood and his precious fiancée. How very interesting. And what a pity for poor Lord Marwood. Poor, dear Lord Marwood, who was obviously still in love with his precious Charlotte and trying to win her back.

Celia's eyes glittered with anticipation. Now, how best to make use of this piece of information which had just fallen into her lap like a gift from the gods? And how to ensure that Miss Kingsley did not take him back, under any circumstances?

"Lady Howard, I believe this is our dance?"

Reluctantly pulled from her scheming, Celia glanced up into Lord Barrymore's face, and breathed a sigh of resignation. Really, the man was such a bore. Marwood probably had it right when he had referred to him as a clunch. He obviously had no more use for him than...

Celia halted in mid thought. *That clunch, Barrymore.* But of course, how stupid of her not to have seen it before. Marwood did not like Barrymore so it was only natural to assume that Barrymore, in turn, would not like Marwood. And if that were the case, Barrymore would probably be only too happy to see the earl's betrothal come to an end. Happy enough to help make it happen?

Slowly the wheels began to turn.

"Why, yes, it is, Lord Barrymore," Celia apologized sincerely. "I hope you will forgive my momentary distraction, but I was entirely flustered by your handsome appearance this evening. Is that, perhaps, a new coat?"

"Yes, er, as a matter of fact, it is."

"I thought so. Indeed, you look every bit as fine as Mr. Brummell himself."

Barrymore gazed down at her in astonishment. "I do?"

Celia placed her gloved hand upon his arm as they began to walk. "I meant to make comment upon it when I first saw you earlier this evening. Although—" she lowered her voice to a more intimate level "—perhaps it has nothing to do with the cut of the jacket. Perhaps it is the man himself who fills the coat so admirably."

Barrymore nearly tripped. He had not missed the imperceptible tightening of Celia's fingers on his arm. Was it possible that she had changed her mind and decided to accept his offer? No time like the present to find out.

"I wonder if you might like to join me for a moonlight stroll through the garden, Lady Howard."

"I should like that very much . . . Fitzhugh. So much more private than being on a crowded dance floor, don't you think?"

Barrymore flushed, all thoughts of the little ballet dancer vanishing. "It certainly is, Lady Howard."

She squeezed his arm again. "Why don't you call me Celia."

Barrymore's chest puffed out to twice its normal size. He could hardly wait to tell that pompous Marwood that the waters had turned very warm, indeed! "It would be my pleasure. Shall we, my dear?"

Celia was careful not to let him see the triumph in her smile as she allowed him to lead her towards the door. *No, my dear Marwood,* Celia smiled smugly to herself, *this is certainly not over yet!*

THE REST OF THE EVENING passed uneventfully enough, though by one o'clock, Charlotte was more than ready to leave. Standing at her side, Marwood noticed her frequent glances towards the door. "Charlotte, would you like me to take you home?"

Charlotte glanced at him through her lashes, a mixture of appreciation and apprehension in her eyes. As much as she was reluctant to share the close confines of the carriage with Devon, neither did she wish to tarry here any longer. The evening had been long enough.

"Yes, thank you, Lord Marwood," Charlotte replied at length. "I should be grateful."

Nodding, Marwood went to fetch their cloaks. He slipped Charlotte's around her shoulders and then escorted her outside to his waiting carriage. Climbing in beside her, he thumped his cane on the roof and they set off at once.

They drove for a while in silence, the clip-clopping of the horses's hooves on the uneven cobbles the only sound in the darkened carriage. Marwood knew that Charlotte was uneasy and purposely steered the conversation away from any discussion of their own situation. He asked instead, "How is your aunt feeling today?"

"Better, my lord." Charlotte slowly let out the breath she had been holding. "In fact, this morning she asked Mrs. Bramble to make up some of her special broth. She swears her herbs are doing more for her than Dr. Palfrey's medicine ever did. I expect that she will be up and about very soon."

"No doubt she is eager to do so." Marwood chuckled affectionately. "I understand the ladies of the ton are also hoping for a swift recovery."

Charlotte smiled reluctantly, bringing into evidence a most charming dimple in her left cheek. "No more than I. My aunt is not the easiest of patients."

Marwood laughed, the sound suddenly bringing Charlotte's other dimple into sight. How she loved to hear Devon laugh. It brought a lightness to his face she had not seen in weeks. Not since...

Charlotte quickly averted her face, not wanting him to see the sudden look of longing in her eyes. What a fool she had been to think that she could so easily dismiss Devon from her heart. She loved him just as much now as she had the day he had proposed.

"You've gone very quiet, Charlotte."

"Have I?" Charlotte fumbled with her reticule. "I was just thinking of...Aunt Kittie again. She was... asking about you this morning."

Marwood's reply came in the form of a deep, throaty chuckle. "Was she, indeed? Well, tell her that I shall stop by within the next day or two and pay her a visit, if she is feeling up to it."

Charlotte's reply was guarded. "I am sure she would be delighted to see you, my lord. It will give her something to look forward to."

Marwood noticed the evasiveness of her answer and added, "And will you look forward to my coming, too, Charlotte?"

Charlotte purposely glanced away. "My lord, I—"

To her surprise, Marwood shook his head and then raised her hand to his lips, pressing a kiss into the palm. It was a tender, lingering kiss, and it shook Charlotte far more than she cared to admit.

"Dear Charlotte," Marwood breathed, releasing her hand before she had cause to reprimand him. "What am I going to do with you?"

But as Charlotte watched him climb back into the carriage after walking her to the front door of her house, thoughts of what he was going to do with her were nowhere near disturbing as thoughts of what she was going to do without him!

"No! I will not take any more of that vile concoction!" Aunt Kittie said, crossing her arms in defiance. "Take it away."

Charlotte fought to keep a lid on her temper. "Dr. Palfrey said you were to take the medicine until it was all gone."

"Fine. Then throw it away and it *will* be all gone."

"Aunt Kittie!"

"Charlotte, I told you, I feel much better."

"But you're not eating enough to keep a bird alive."

"Hmph!" Aunt Kittie glanced towards the maid. "Anna? Run down to the kitchen and have Mrs. Bramble give you the blue bottle on the window ledge." She smiled at her niece sweetly. "Nothing like a bit of ginger tonic to help restore the appetite—which I probably lost as a direct result of Palfrey's medicine!"

Charlotte tapped her foot in agitation. "Aunt Kittie, I vow you are the worst patient."

"Then leave me be to cure myself." Aunt Kittie regarded her niece mumpishly. "My herbs have never hurt me before."

Charlotte rose from her seat beside the bed. "May I remind you that it was your blasted herbs that put you here in the first place. If you weren't so stubborn about storing those heavy jars on top of the wardrobe—"

"The oils have to mature, Charlotte," Aunt Kittie told her. "They must not be disturbed—"

"What must not be disturbed?" Edward asked from the doorway.

"Edward, thank goodness you have come. Charlotte was just chastising me again." Aunt Kittie lifted her cheek for her nephew's kiss. "Perhaps your arrival will spare me another tongue-lashing."

"Hmm, I don't know about that," Edward told her. "Seems to me I should be adding my voice to Charlotte's. From what Lotte has told me, Aunt Catherine, this isn't the first time she has caught you lugging those heavy jars around." He grinned engagingly. "Why can't you find a safer hobby?"

"Hobby! This is not a hobby, my dear boy, this is important work! A lot of people depend on my knowledge of herbs and flowers. There would be a great many disappointed ladies were I to suddenly put an end to my production."

"*They* might be disappointed, but *I* know I should sleep better," Charlotte grumbled.

Edward glanced at his sister in amusement. "Perhaps what we need to do is come up with a better way of storing your jars."

"Somewhere they won't be moved around," Aunt Kittie was quick to point out. "Movement disturbs the aging. And some of them must be matured in the dark."

"Fine. Why don't we extend the back kitchen and you can store them on the floor? That way, there will be no need for you to carry the bottles up the stairs or move them on and off the top of your wardrobe."

Aunt Kittie began to look hopeful. "Edward, I think that might be just the thing! Yes, Dickens?"

"Excuse me, Miss Harper, but Lady Howard is downstairs. She would like to pay her respects, if you are feeling up to it."

Charlotte's brows drew together. "Lady Howard? How very strange. I wonder why she would be calling." She turned to regard her aunt. "I don't believe she has ever stopped in before."

Aunt Kittie's concern, however, was for an entirely different matter. "Oh, dear, a visitor, and just look at me, will you. Anna, see what you can do with my hair." Aunt Kittie glanced at her reflection in the looking-glass opposite the bed and poked her fingers ineffectually through her hair. "Looks like birds have been nesting. Quick, fetch my lace cap. The newest one. And my shawl."

Charlotte turned towards the door. "Come, Teddy, Anna has her work cut out for her here, and I daresay we have ours." She linked her arm in her brother's. "Society is beating a path to our door. I fear your self-imposed isolation is about to come to an end."

In the drawing-room, Charlotte found Lady Howard admiring a set of hunting prints over the fireplace. Her pelisse of soft merino wool was both stylish and flattering to her voluptuous figure, making Charlotte suddenly very conscious of her own rather slender build. "Good afternoon, Lady Howard."

Lady Howard turned at the sound of her arrival. She had been planning this visit to Miss Kingsley since the night of Lady Wilton's soirée, and knew exactly what she was going to say. She opened her mouth to begin with the usual insincere words of greeting, but stopped rather abruptly, as her eyes lit on the tall handsome man standing beside Charlotte. "Oh, forgive me, Miss Kingsley, I was not aware that you already had... company."

There was no mistaking the interest in her gaze or the implication in her voice. Charlotte blushed and said quickly, "Lady Howard, may I present my brother, Edward."

Celia's eyes widened even further. "Your brother! Ah, so this is the illustrious gentleman of whom I have heard so much. Welcome home, Mr. Kingsley. How does it feel to be a returning hero?''

Edward smiled, but his eyes were cool. "I'm sure I do not know, Lady Howard, since I hardly think of myself as one. I only did what I had to do."

Lady Howard brushed aside his modesty. "I understand you did far more than that, Mr. Kingsley, but your humility does you credit, nevertheless."

Edward inclined his head in acknowledgement, averting his eyes from the woman's forthright regard.

"I . . . understand you wished to see my aunt, Lady Howard," Charlotte said.

"Yes." Celia reluctantly dragged her eyes away from Edward. "I heard some of the ladies discussing Miss Harper's unfortunate accident at Lady Wilton's the other evening and thought it only polite to stop in and see how she fares."

"That is most kind of you. I know my aunt will welcome the diversion." Charlotte turned towards her brother. "Edward, are you coming up?"

"No, Charlotte, if you don't mind I won't join you," Edward said. "I was just on my way out when Lady Howard arrived." He turned to regard their visitor. "It was a pleasure meeting you, Lady Howard."

"The pleasure was all mine, Mr. Kingsley, though I hope we shall soon be seeing you out in Society." Lady Howard's voice dropped to a throaty purr. "It would be a shame to deprive all the lovely young ladies of your company."

Edward smiled pleasantly. "I am sure the ladies will survive." He winked at Charlotte and turned to go. "See you later, Lotte."

Charlotte hastily averted her face, her lips twitching. "If you will follow me, Lady Howard." She turned to lead the way up to her aunt's room.

Celia followed thoughtfully. "What a charming brother you have, Miss Kingsley. Quite charming, indeed."

The visit lasted no more than ten minutes, though not owing to any weariness on Aunt Kittie's part. Lady Howard barely seemed to have sat down before she was rising to say her goodbyes. She declined both Charlotte's offer of refreshments and her aunt's offer of tea.

Hiding her surprise, Charlotte dutifully accompanied her guest back downstairs.

"I apologize that I cannot stay longer, Miss Kingsley," Celia said when they reached the bottom of the stairs, "but I do have a few other calls to make, and you know how quickly the time goes."

Charlotte smiled. "It was good of you to stop by at all, Lady Howard. I am sure my aunt was happy to see a new face."

Lady Howard watched her with interest. "And what about you, Miss Kingsley? I am sure you could use a friendly face right now, or perhaps a sympathetic ear."

Charlotte smiled politely. "I beg your pardon?"

Lady Howard offered her a glance filled with pity. "Come now, Miss Kingsley, there is really no need to pretend. I am aware that all is not well between you and Lord Marwood."

Charlotte flushed. "Lady Howard, I really—"

"Now, you needn't worry, your secret is safe with me. I am a woman of the world, and I know that sometimes things do not work out quite the way we hope they will." She paused for effect. "Devon was most disturbed when he was talking to me about it."

Charlotte stared at her visitor in shock. "He...spoke to you of this?"

Celia avoided the question in such a way as to make it appear that she was reluctant to answer. "You must understand, Miss Kingsley, that in times of unhappiness, men will be men. They are not as strong as women, for all their displays of bravado. They often seek out the company and advice of an old friend. Someone with whom they have been ... close." Lady Howard's glance suddenly became very intent. "You do understand what I am saying, don't you, Miss Kingsley?"

Charlotte's chin lifted. "I am not sure that I do, Lady Howard."

Celia's smile was reminiscent of a cat who had just discovered a nest full of mice. "You will, in time. Good afternoon, Miss Kingsley."

Charlotte stood staring at the door long after her visitor had gone, more shaken than she cared to admit. Eventually, she turned and walked into the yellow salon, mulling over mind the strange conversation which had just taken place.

Devon had gone to Lady Howard about their problems? No, it was entirely too ridiculous to be believed, Charlotte decided. Devon would not tell anyone of their contretemps just yet. Not until she had given him leave to. There was Aunt Kittie's health to consider, after all.

And yet, how else could Lady Howard have known that she and Devon were at odds? And what did she mean by saying that Devon had sought out the company of an old friend? Was Lady Howard insinuating that Devon had renewed his association with her, and that he had told her of their problems as a result?

Charlotte sat down in the wing-backed chair, frowning in annoyance. She was suddenly sure of one thing. There was only one reason why Lady Howard had come to the house today—and it had absolutely nothing to do with Aunt Kittie's welfare!

CHAPTER NINE

"YOU'RE LOOKING very pleased with yourself," Lord Barrymore said as he helped Celia climb back into the closed carriage. He thumped his cane on the roof. "Set the cat amongst the pigeons, have you?"

Lady Howard smiled as they set off. "I certainly have, my dear Fitz. The seeds of doubt have been planted and now require a little watering."

"And that's where I come in."

Celia nodded. She had known from the start that Barrymore would help her. It had required little more than a harmless fondle in a darkened garden to ensure his cooperation. "Did you get the coat?"

"An almost exact copy, and at a considerably reduced price." Barrymore grinned. "A friend of mine owed me a little favour. Tossed in the hat, as well."

"Good. It is fortunate that you and Marwood are of a like build. From a distance, it will certainly appear as though you are the earl, even though Miss Kingsley will only be given a brief glimpse of you."

Barrymore's smile was little more than a sneer. "I take it Miss Kingsley is not going to be left in any doubt as to the identity of the lady with Lord Marwood."

Celia smiled. "No doubt at all. And what she will see us doing is going to make her very unhappy, indeed."

Barrymore frowned. "But what if she doesn't come to the Park? How you do you know she will believe the letter?"

Celia idly ran her hand along his leg, feeling him tense. "Curiosity, my dear Fitz. After our little talk just now, there is no doubt in my mind that Miss Kingsley will come, if for no other reason than to see if her beloved Marwood really is seeing me again. And if things are as bad as I suspect between them, it will not take much to estrange them completely. I rather imagine the sight of Devon in a passionate embrace with his former mistress should be enough to do it."

Barrymore gloated. "Do you know, I shall enjoy seeing Marwood made to look a fool when everyone discovers that Miss Kingsley has turned him down flat. It will serve him bloody well right!"

Celia's cat-like smile spread. She, too, would enjoy seeing Marwood's betrothal come to an end, though certainly not for the same reasons as Barrymore.

When the walls of Devon's engagement came crashing down, Celia intended to be there to pick up the pieces, and to offer the poor man comfort in the best way she knew how.

MARWOOD SAT in the drawing-room of the house in Grosvenor Square, one booted ankle crossed over the other, and stared into the flames of the fire Robertson had started. The book on his lap lay open to the page he had begun an hour ago. Only one thing occupied his mind right now. Charlotte Kingsley—and what he was going to do without her.

"So, I find you plunged into the depths of despair again," Longworth teased him from the doorway. "Getting to be a bit of a habit, old boy."

Marwood glanced up, obviously surprised to see the viscount leaning negligently against the door, and then turned back to the sight of the flames crackling in the fireplace. "I fear I shall have to reprimand my butler," Marwood muttered. "I specifically told him I was not at home to visitors."

Longworth chuckled and sauntered forward, draping his lanky form over the arm of a nearby chair. "Ah, but therein lies the difference, Marwood. I am not a visitor. I am a friend, and one who cares enough to brave the stones that are occasionally hurled at my head."

Longworth glanced at the earl, his gaze quickly taking in the half-empty brandy decanter on the table and the look of resignation on the noble features. "I take it the course of love is still not running smoothly?"

Marwood's response was little more than a grunt. "At the moment, the road to love is plagued with more twists and turns than a donkey's hind leg."

"Never mind, Dev, I've brought someone to help cheer you up."

"Thank you, I am not in a mood to socialize."

"Nevertheless, this is someone I think you should meet."

"Longworth, if I have to tell—"

"Good evening, sir," a voice said pleasantly. "Have I at long last the honour of addressing Lord Marwood?"

There was a brief silence as Marwood rose and turned towards the door. His recognition of the man was instantaneous. "Good Lord! Edward Kingsley."

Longworth slanted him an amused glance. "I told you."

Marwood slowly began to smile. "I am honoured, sir, though I confess you have taken me somewhat by surprise."

Edward advanced and the two men shook hands. "I apologize that we have not been able to meet sooner, Lord Marwood, but I have been keeping to myself since my return. Poor Charlotte has been nearly beside herself trying to arrange a meeting between us."

"Yes, so I understand," Marwood replied evasively. "Still, the fault is as much mine as yours." He indicated the chair beside his own. "Can I offer you something to drink? Cognac, perhaps? Or would you prefer a port?"

Edward chuckled. "Cognac will be fine. One of the few pleasant memories I have of my time in France is of downing a bottle or two of particularly fine brandy. Made me forget where I was for a few hours."

Longworth winked devilishly at Edward. "I told you we would catch him off guard." Then, to Marwood, "I thought it was about time the three of us got together, Dev, considering the common bond we share."

"Yes, of course." Marwood handed a glass each to Edward and Nicholas. "A toast on the successful completion of your mission, Kingsley, and to your safe return home. You must be very glad it's all over."

"I am, indeed, relieved to be back on English soil," Edward confessed, "though I am sure it is a feeling you know well enough yourself."

Marwood smiled, warming to the man. "Yes, I do recall having felt that way once or twice, though the memory is fading somewhat. I have not been active in the service these past few years."

"Nevertheless, I've heard Lord Osborne speak of you frequently, and always with the utmost respect." Edward's mouth curved in a knowing grin. "He was sorry to lose you, Lord Marwood, though I can well understand your reasons for resigning. Family obligations and all that."

"Speaking of which, how is Miss Harper coming along?" Longworth enquired.

"Very well, and I understand I am in your debt, Lord Marwood, for acting so swiftly on her behalf. You have my thanks, sir."

Marwood shrugged off the compliment, though his lips quivered slightly. "Miss Harper is an endearing lady. I should not like to see anything happen to her."

"My sentiments exactly."

Longworth picked up the conversation again. "I have been telling Edward that you are a reasonable swordsman, Dev. I think he fancies having a go at you."

Marwood looked at Edward in surprise. "Do you fence?"

Edward grinned. "I haven't for a long time, though I would welcome the opportunity of trying my hand again. Perhaps we could arrange to meet for a bout sometime?"

"I would be delighted," Marwood replied without hesitation. "Shall we say ten o'clock at O'Shaunessy's, the day after tomorrow?"

"Ten o'clock will be fine." Edward studied the man in front of him for a few minutes and then nodded. "I know I have left the most important issue until last, Lord Marwood, but I should like to say how very pleased I am that you and Charlotte are to be wed. Charlotte is very special to me and I am glad to see that she has chosen so wisely." He held out his hand. "I shall be honoured to have you in the family, my lord."

Marwood glanced at the outstretched hand, and hesitated. Out of the corner of his eye, he saw Nicholas shake his head. Marwood smoothly accepted Edward's hand and replied. "No happier than I will be, I can assure you."

"Right, now that all the introductions and polite chit-chat have been taken care of," Longworth remarked, rising, "what say we head over to the Clarendon for some dinner. I, for one, am devilishly hungry."

Marwood glanced over at Edward. "Are you engaged to dine, sir?"

Edward shrugged. "I had no particular plans, my lord."

"Splendid!" Longworth said. "Then let us be off. I've heard the chef's *côtelettes d'agneau* are exceptionally fine."

Marwood glanced at Edward. "I hope Charlotte will not be upset that you are not dining at home with her."

"I shouldn't imagine so. I did say before I left that I was not sure what my plans were for this evening. Besides, she may appreciate a few quiet hours alone. Now that Aunt Catherine is recovering, she will be receiving a lot of visitors. Lady Howard dropped by this afternoon."

"Celia?" Longworth could barely contain his surprise. "Good heavens, I didn't think she had a charitable bone in her body."

"Well, I must admit, I did find the lady rather... forward," Edward remarked as tactfully as he could.

Marwood finished off his brandy. "Forward is a kind way of putting it, Kingsley. Lady Howard has all the compassion of a jackal. Something tells me if she was there, it wasn't solely to see your aunt."

"My money is on her wanting to see *you*," Long-worth piped up. "Everyone knows that Celia is monu-mentally curious."

"Curious is not the only thing Celia is known for be-ing," Marwood pointed out drily. "But come, enough of this gossiping. Let us repair to the Clarendon. I un-derstand they also do an exceptionally fine *filet de boeuf à la napolitaine !*"

Edward laughed and likewise rose to his feet. "I hope you will forgive me if I do *not* order a serving of that!"

"EDWARD, ARE YOU READY?" Charlotte called up the stairs. "I have left it as late as I dare."

"Lotte, if you don't want to attend the thing in the first place, why are you bothering to go?" Edward asked with typical male logic. "Surely you are not ex-pected to attend every function for which you receive an invitation."

"Certainly not, but one is expected to try." Char-lotte smiled as she watched her brother descend the stairs. "Lady Broughton is a very influential member of Society, and one cannot run the risk of offending her. Besides which, she is a dreadful gossip, and if I do not appear I shall probably end up being the topic of dis-cussion at this afternoon's tea."

"Egad, a fate worse than death, and one to be avoided at all costs," Edward teased her. "Do you know, Lotte, I am sometimes grateful for my absence over the past three years. At least it kept me out of the drawing-rooms of Society without causing a great deal of speculation as to why."

"True, Edward," Charlotte sighed. "At times, I wish I might have been so fortunate."

Edward glanced at his sister. "And why would a happily betrothed young lady such as yourself wish to avoid mixing in polite Society? When you are the Countess of Marwood, you will be a much-acclaimed hostess and one well able to get back at these ladies who strike such fear into your gallant little heart now. Speaking of which, where is the dashing Lord Marwood this afternoon? Should he not be arriving to escort you himself?"

Affecting a casual air, Charlotte attended to an errant curl which had somehow slipped out from under her elegant new bonnet. "Lord Marwood does not particularly enjoy affairs of this nature, Teddy, though he did say he would try to put in an appearance a little later."

"I see. Well, I am very glad that, if nothing else, I have finally had occasion to meet the illustrious gentleman."

Charlotte froze. "You met Devon? When?"

"Last evening. Longworth was good enough to introduce us. The three of us had dinner at the Clarendon." Edward turned to study his own impeccably arranged cravat. "He is a fine man, Lotte. I like him very much. I can see why you wanted us to meet. By the by, when are you going to set the date?"

Edward's words, so innocently spoken, were almost her undoing, and Charlotte had to bite her lip to keep from telling him the truth. Thank goodness Devon had not told him. She did not want Edward to know what was going on just yet. She wanted him settled in his life first. Then and only then would she tell him that there had been a misunderstanding.

Instead, Charlotte drew a deep breath and pasted a brilliant smile on her face. "Soon, Edward. But come, let us be off. Lady Broughton awaits."

The afternoon traffic was light and they made good time to Lady Broughton's large, impressive house on the outskirts of Town. Edward brought the carriage to a halt in front of the imposing gates and climbed down to help Charlotte alight. She gave him a smile bright with encouragement. "Ready, Edward?"

Edward took a deep breath and nodded, not at all sure that he was. "As I will ever be, I suppose. Lead on, Lotte."

In the drawing-room, Lady Broughton greeted them with open arms and an expression of unfeigned delight. "Charlotte, how very charming you look this afternoon. And Edward, dear boy, welcome home. How wonderful to see you safely back in England. I cannot tell you how honoured I am that you have chosen my humble gathering as your vehicle to re-enter Society." She lowered her voice to a whisper. "I know that Lady Roxton was most disappointed that you did not choose hers." Then louder, "Ladies, gentlemen, look who has joined us. Our returning hero, Edward Kingsley!"

Charlotte bit her lip as all eyes turned to regard them. She saw the flush steal over her brother's firm chin and up into his cheeks. This was definitely not what he had been expecting. He smiled bravely, however, as the crowd began to surge towards him.

"I will get you back for this, Lotte," Edward whispered out of the side of his mouth.

Charlotte struggled to contain her laughter. "All hail the conquering hero," she whispered back. "Welcome to Society, Teddy."

As Edward was swallowed up in the crowd, Charlotte found herself gently pushed aside. How quickly the focus of attention shifted in the world of the *beau monde*, she reflected. Still, it was probably a blessing in disguise. In the excitement of Edward's appearance, at least Devon's absence had gone unnoticed.

Almost.

"And where is your handsome fiancée this afternoon, Miss Kingsley?" Lady Broughton enquired. "I understood that he was coming."

"Unfortunately, Lord Marwood was... otherwise engaged, Lady Broughton," Charlotte heard herself respond in an overly bright tone. "He did say that if time allowed, he would try to stop in later."

"Well, I can only hope that he will, of course. It would have been nice to see all of you together at last." Lady Broughton watched Edward dealing with his new-found prominence, content in the knowledge that she had achieved a social coup. "I am surprised that your brother was so reluctant to return to Society, though. He seems to be handling it very well. Was he just shy?"

"Actually, my brother has been very busy since his return, Lady Broughton. He has not had a great deal of time to spare for such things."

"I should think not," Lord Barrymore said, joining them unexpectedly. "Probably been spending time at Carlton House. Man's a hero. Genuine out-and-outer."

"Yes, and quite outrageously handsome, too." Lady Howard, who had arrived on Barrymore's arm, slid her eyes towards Charlotte significantly. "Almost as handsome as your fiancé, Miss Kingsley."

Charlotte felt the colour rise to her cheeks and was thankful for the timely arrival of more guests. She took advantage of the opportunity to slip away from Lady

Howard and Lord Barrymore. Really, the woman was too forward, Charlotte fumed inwardly. First Devon and now Edward. Even Lord Barrymore seemed to be hanging all over her. Did the woman spare no time for her husband?

Eventually, Edward managed to disentangle himself from the throng and slowly worked his way back to Charlotte's side. His expression was anything but pleased. "By Jove, have I really been away that long or has my memory dimmed?"

Charlotte tried not to smile. "In what regard, Teddy? Are you not enjoying the attention of the ladies?"

"I feel like a prize stallion up for bid at Tattersall's," he grumbled.

"Dear me, that bad, was it?"

"All they had left to do was check my teeth."

"Oh, dear!" Charlotte laughed. "No, doubt they would have, given time."

"Lotte, this is not funny!" Edward retorted. He went to continue, then stopped, his frown quickly changing to a smile. "Why, Miss Beaufort, I had not realized that you were here."

Laura laughed prettily. "It is hardly surprising, Mr. Kingsley, considering the way you were set upon the moment you stepped through the door. Society has been anxious to welcome you home."

Edward stifled a sigh. "Yes, so I have discovered."

Laura glanced up at him coquettishly. "Are you not pleased by the attention?"

"I fear not. It was only Charlotte's pleading that made me come at all this afternoon."

"Then I must thank Charlotte for doing such a good job," Laura replied softly.

For the first time that afternoon, Edward actually looked glad that he had come. "Perhaps it was worth it, Miss Beaufort, if for no other reason than to hear you say so. You are looking very lovely this afternoon." His gaze dropped to the familiar shawl around her shoulders. "It becomes you."

Laura blushed. "It was very kind of you to purchase it for me, Mr. Kingsley, though I am not at all sure I should accept such an extravagant gift."

"But why not? I only bought it because you did not have time to." Edward directed a speaking glance at Charlotte. "As I recall, we had to leave the shop in rather a hurry. Something about a three o'clock visit, wasn't it, Charlotte?"

Charlotte tapped him playfully on the arm. "Now, don't bring that up again, Teddy. Laura has forgiven me for my innocent meddling, haven't you, Laura?"

Laura tried to look stern, but failed. "Yes, of course I have."

"There, you see, Edward. Laura has no—" Charlotte broke off as she saw another set of new arrivals turn to regard them. "Oh, dear, I think you are about to be set upon again, Edward. I see Lady Broughton pointing this way. Come Laura, let us leave Edward to his adoring public."

The girls did exactly that as Edward stoically went to meet the newest arrivals. Laura turned back to watch him with a smile.

"Poor Edward. He must be finding all this quite tedious. He does not seem the type to enjoy such attention."

Charlotte's eyes sparkled mischievously. "He loathes it. He was not exaggerating when he said I practically had to drag him here today."

"Well, I am very glad that you did. Your brother is the sweetest, kindest, most wonderful man I have ever met."

Charlotte smiled. "And you are terribly in love with him, aren't you?"

Laura blushed crimson. "Oh, dear, does it show so very much?"

Charlotte laughed and pressed Laura's arm affectionately. "Only when you talk about him."

"Is your brother still involved in . . . business, Charlotte?" Laura asked carefully.

"I fear so. It is one of the things you may want to consider if you hope to marry Edward."

"Marry him!" It was clear that Laura did not know whether to laugh, blush or just feign innocence. Somehow, her response managed to combine all three. "I would hardly dare to be so presumptuous. Oh, bother!" she said, suddenly noticing a girl waving to her from the corner. "Marianne Bradbourne is after me again. No doubt to ask questions about your brother or your fiancé."

"Why don't you just pretend that you did not see her?" Charlotte suggested.

"Because if I do that, she will tell everyone that I slighted her. Never mind, I shall give her some vague answers and leave it at that. I'll see you before you leave."

Squaring her shoulders, Laura walked away. Unfortunately, as soon as she did, Lady Howard moved in. "There you are, Miss Kingsley, I have been wanting to speak with you for an age, but it is so difficult to get you alone. I vow you are almost as popular as your brother."

"Nowhere near as popular, I shouldn't think, Lady Howard. If you will excuse—"

"But why are you in such a hurry to leave, Miss Kingsley? I only came over to pay my compliments on the splendid job you are doing."

Charlotte hesitated. "I beg your pardon?"

"Yes, you play your part in a most convincing manner." Celia smiled complacently. "I doubt anyone in this room would guess that things have altered significantly between you and Lord Marwood."

Charlotte stood her ground admirably. "I really do not know what you are talking about. Now if you don't mind—"

"Ah, but I think you do, Miss Kingsley," Celia said quickly, "though I confess, I do not understand the reason behind your game. If you and Lord Marwood are no longer betrothed, why are you trying to pretend that you are?"

Charlotte stopped, aware of a horrible, sinking feeling in the pit of her stomach. There was no way the woman could have known that. She might have been able to hazard a guess as to the state of her relationship with Devon, but there was no way she could have known that the betrothal was at an end. Only Charlotte and four other people knew that, three of whom had been sworn to silence. Which only left Devon.

Reasons notwithstanding, Charlotte decided to fight fire with fire. "You seem uncommonly interested in what is going on between myself and Lord Marwood. Is there any particular reason?"

"But of course. Have you forgotten what I said the other day?"

Her smile held a wealth of meaning, and seeing it, Charlotte lifted her chin. "I saw no reason to remember it."

Celia tutted and shook her head. "Miss Kingsley, why are you trying to make this more difficult for yourself. It would be a great deal simpler if you just admitted that it was over and let him go on his way."

"You presume a great deal, Lady Howard," Charlotte said coldly.

"Not really. There is no point in being sentimental about these things, Miss Kingsley, especially as it will all come out soon enough. Besides, who do you think you are fooling?" Celia asked. "Devon is a man of the world. He enjoys what life has to offer. And if the two of you are not to be wed, what is there to stop him from taking his pleasures where he wishes?" Celia glanced at her with pity. "Why don't you just . . . let him go?"

"Why? So that he might come back to you?" Charlotte enquired bitterly.

Celia's thin smile flashed. "My poor dear Charlotte, you really don't know, do you. He already has come back to me. How do you think I know the truth about your betrothal? Did you believe I just plucked it out of thin air?"

Charlotte gasped. "I don't believe you! Devon would not—" Charlotte abruptly broke off as the hairs on the back of her neck began to rise. Devon was standing in the doorway—and looking straight at her.

Celia saw him, too. "Perhaps it would be better if I were to leave the two of you alone," she said quickly. "No doubt you have much to say to one another."

Charlotte flushed. Against her will, her eyes were drawn back to the man standing in the doorway. She did not notice Celia slip away. She was aware only of Devon watching her. She saw his eyes travel slowly over her and blushed at his openly admiring gaze.

At the other side of the room, Lady Broughton could scarcely conceal her delight. "Why, Lord Marwood, how splendid that you could join us. Charlotte said that you probably would not be here until later. Charlotte, look who has arrived!"

The remark quite naturally drew attention to Marwood's arrival, and a number of heads turned, curious as to why the Earl of Marwood and his fiancée had arrived at yet another function separately. Charlotte smiled and walked towards him, knowing there was nothing else she could do.

Devon noticed her stiffness immediately. "Good evening, Charlotte."

"My lord." Her tone was unintentionally sharp, and Charlotte felt the inquisitive eyes of her hostess upon her. She forced herself to adopt a more affectionate tone. "I am surprised to see you here so early. Your business obviously concluded sooner than you had led me to believe."

Marwood's performance was faultless. "Much sooner, in fact. Had I but known, I would have picked you up as we had originally planned. However, since I knew that Edward was bringing you, I felt secure in the knowledge that I would see you once I arrived."

His performance did not end there. To Charlotte's dismay, he lifted her hand to his lips and pressed a gentle kiss against it. It was as much as she could do not to flinch.

The sentimental gesture, however, seemed to satisfy the eyes and the ears of the curious. Charlotte noticed a table of ladies return their attention to their cards as the general hum of conversation resumed. As Lady

Broughton moved away, Devon stepped closer. "What was Celia saying to you when I came in?"

Charlotte started, but did not meet his eyes. "Lady Howard? Nothing. Why?"

"No reason. I just thought you were looking rather upset. I wondered if she had said something to disturb you."

Charlotte finally swivelled her gaze round to his. "Is there something she might say that you would prefer I not hear, Lord Marwood?"

"Not at all, but Celia can be rather difficult at times," he told her bluntly.

Charlotte laughed mirthlessly. "You should know that better than I."

Marwood carefully held on to his temper. "And what is that supposed to mean?"

"Nothing, except that it appears that I was not in possession of all the facts the other evening when I asked you if you had been involved with her."

"What other facts? Charlotte, I—"

"Why, Lord Marwood, what a pleasure to see you," Edward said, arriving at their side. "Charlotte led me to believe you would not be attending this afternoon. Had I but known, I would have allowed you to come in my place."

Marwood smiled lazily. "Are you not enjoying your return to Society, Mr. Kingsley?"

"I am finding it something of an eye-opener, my lord," Edward commented ruefully. "But it is, as I am well aware, something which had to be undertaken sooner or later. Are we still on for tomorrow morning?"

"We are, but I fear I shall have to make it an hour later. Will that pose a problem for you?"

Edward shook his head. "Not in the least."

"Good. I shall send word to Lord Longworth."

"Edward, I wonder if you are ready to leave?" Charlotte interrupted. She purposely avoided Devon's gaze. "I did tell Aunt Kittie that I would spend some time with her this afternoon, and the hour is getting on."

"Yes, I rather think I am," said Edward. "Can I offer you a ride home, Marwood?"

"Thank you, but my phaeton is outside."

"Well, I shall leave you two alone to say your goodbyes."

"That will not be necessary, Edward," Charlotte said swiftly. "Lord Marwood and I have already said all we need to say to one another. Good afternoon." Without a second glance, Charlotte abruptly turned on her heel and left.

Watching her, Marwood's eyes narrowed thoughtfully. Something had happened to upset Charlotte this afternoon, and he strongly suspected it involved Celia. He glanced around the room and spotted her chatting with Lord Barrymore. *What a pair,* Marwood thought dispassionately as he made his way across the floor. *The spider and the serpent, comparing notes.*

"Good afternoon, Lady Howard. Barrymore."

The two looked round at his greeting. Barrymore's acknowledgement was cool at best, Celia's considerably more sociable. "Well, Lord Marwood. This is an unexpected pleasure." Her voice was like warm honey. "You do not normally trouble yourself to seek me out. At least, not anymore," she could not resist adding.

Marwood's smile didn't reach his eyes. "I wonder if I might have a word with you, Lady Howard. In private."

Celia's laughter issued from deep in her throat. "You may have anything you wish with me in private, Devon, you know that."

Beside her, Barrymore coughed. "If you will excuse me."

Marwood waited until the man moved off before returning his attention to Celia. "Your taste has deteriorated, Celia."

She pouted prettily. "You left me little choice, Devon. There is no one in the ton to compare with you."

"I understand you have been quite thorough in your attempts to find someone who was."

Celia did not blush, though the significance of his words was not lost upon her. "Do not scold, Devon, I am married to an old man who finds a great deal more pleasure in his books and his bottle than he does in me."

Marwood raised one eyebrow meaningfully. "You should have thought of that before you married him."

Celia shrugged eloquently. "There were extenuating circumstances. After all, the match was not without its financial compensations. My husband is most generous with my allowance, and pretty much turns a blind eye to what I do with it. And there is the title."

Marwood's reply was carefully circumspect. "I'm sure many women would envy you."

"Would they?" Celia glanced up at him boldly "Would Miss Kingsley, I wonder?"

Marwood refused to be drawn. "Speaking of my fiancée, I noticed you talking with Charlotte when I arrived, and that she seemed rather distressed."

"Did she?" Celia slid her gaze away from his, as though wearied of the conversation. "What is that to me?"

"Did you say something to upset her?"

"My dear Marwood, what could I have possibly said to upset the girl?"

"I don't know, but I warn you, Celia—" Marwood's voice dropped "—if I find out that you have, you will not escape lightly. I intend to marry Charlotte Kingsley, and nothing you say or do is going to change that."

"Really?" He saw a momentary flash of anger in the emerald eyes. "Then I wish you much happiness, my lord."

It was tantamount to a dismissal, and accepting it as such, Marwood bowed curtly and moved away. He took his leave of Lady Broughton almost immediately thereafter.

Watching his exit, Barrymore returned to join Lady Howard, quietly applauding. "Bravo, my dear, a masterful performance."

Celia's head snapped round. "You were eavesdropping?"

Barrymore did not trouble himself to appear apologetic. "I thought it in my best interests to know what was going on, given that I, too, have a part in this little melodrama. Am I to assume that the curtain has fallen on Act Two?"

Celia relaxed slightly. "Yes, I think you may safely assume so." Her calculating smile slowly reappeared. "Leaving the stage suitably set for the third and final act."

CHAPTER TEN

THE LETTER arrived at Green Street that evening.

It was addressed to Miss Charlotte Kingsley, and was slipped under the door by an unseen hand. It lay on the floor in the hall, until Dickens, picking it up and glancing at it rather quizzically, placed it on the silver salver and took it in to Charlotte in the drawing-room.

"A letter for you, Miss Charlotte," he said.

Charlotte glanced up at her butler in surprise. "At this time of night?"

"I found it lying on the floor in the hall, miss," Dickens replied regretfully. "I have no idea how it came to be there, nor who delivered it."

Strange, Charlotte reflected, taking the letter. Who would call and not make himself known? Charlotte looked down at the missive in her hand. There was no indication who might have sent it.

Curious, she broke the seal and unfolded the single sheet of parchment. As she quickly scanned the contents, Charlotte's hand began to tremble as she read the words aloud.

Be warned. He, whom you thought true, will keep a lovers' rendezvous in the Park at dawn.

A lovers' rendezvous?

Charlotte read the note again, turning it over in the

hopes of gaining some clue about its origin. It was printed in block letters so there was no way of determining whether the writer was male or female. There was no address and no signature. It was simply signed, "a friend."

A friend? What kind of friend would send a letter like this and not sign his or her name?

Charlotte stood up, suddenly finding herself too disturbed to remain seated. The letter might, of course, be nothing more than a prank. Charlotte knew there were enough feeble-minded people who would think such a lark amusing. But what if it were not? What if it had been sent to her by someone who had learned that her fiancé was seeing another woman? After all, only she and Devon knew the truth about their betrothal. Perhaps Devon had already taken up with someone behind her back. Was that the purpose behind the note? To make Charlotte believe that her fiancé could be unfaithful? Or to warn her that he already had been?

Whatever the reason, there was certainly no mistaking the intent behind the letter. Someone wanted her to know that Devon was meeting another woman. And at the moment, Charlotte had no reason to believe that the woman would be anyone other than Lady Howard!

THE FIRST PALE PINK fingers of light were just beginning to curl over the horizon as Charlotte cantered her mare along the leafy green trails of Hyde Park. She glanced round the deserted grounds and shivered slightly under the heavy folds of her cape. How cold and uninviting the place seemed. The ground was heavily coated with dew, and the dampness in the air seeped through Charlotte's kid gloves.

Still, she hadn't come here for her own pleasure, Charlotte reminded herself briskly. She had come to witness a lovers' tryst, and it was true enough that early morning was the only time such a meeting could take place. At the commencement of the fashionable hour, the Park would be crowded with people anxious to see and be seen.

Turning in the direction of the Serpentine, Charlotte slowed her mare to a trot, so deep in her own thoughts that she momentarily forgot her reasons for being there in the first place. She was remembering how she and Devon had used to ride along these very paths early in the morning, racing their horses side by side until almost at the end, Devon would press his great black stallion for that extra burst of speed and cross the finish line a nose ahead! What blissful days those had been.

But they were gone now, Charlotte acknowledged sadly. While Devon was still in her life out of necessity, the trust and the love they had once shared was not.

"Men!" Charlotte whispered under her breath. "What fools we are to love them, Lady."

The high, unmistakable whinny of a stallion suddenly drew Charlotte's attention, and she abruptly pulled on the reins, causing Lady to toss her head in protest. Guiltily loosening her hold, Charlotte strained her eyes in the direction of the sound. It was difficult to pick out anything in the dim light.

Then, she saw them; a pair of riders well off in the distance. They were almost hidden from view by the low overhanging branches of a large clump of trees, but there was no mistaking that it was indeed a man and woman.

The woman was dressed in a long flowing cloak, the hood pulled up over her head. The man, whose back was towards Charlotte, wore a distinctive black, multi-caped coat and a wide-brimmed hat pulled down low over his eyes. He rode a black stallion, and sat tall and straight in the saddle, and even though his face was turned away from her, Charlotte recognized something painfully familiar in the set of the powerfully built shoulders.

"Devon?"

Her breath left a misty question in the air, her voice trailing away as she watched the man lean forward and kiss the woman full upon the lips. It was a passionate, lingering kiss, and in spite of her obscurity, Charlotte looked away, feeling herself an intruder in a lovers' tryst. A tryst between an unknown lady and the man she had been going to marry!

Glancing back, she was just in time to see the pair draw apart. Suddenly, the lady's hood suddenly slipped back, revealing features which could belong to no other.

"Lady Howard!"

Charlotte drew a ragged breath and closed her eyes against the sight of that face. She felt the salty sting of tears on her cheeks and the agonizing pain of betrayal rip through her heart. She quickly turned Lady's head around and galloped off in the direction from which she had come.

She had seen all that she needed to see. The letter had not been a fraud. The man she had been in love with was.

LONGWORTH AND Marwood were preparing for their match when Edward Kingsley arrived. Spotting him in the doorway, Longworth grinned and nudged the earl.

"There you see, Marwood, I told you Kingsley wouldn't frighten that easily. Word of your fencing prowess obviously hasn't reached as far as France. Morning, Kingsley," Longworth called as Edward approached. "I hope you've come to take this fellow down a peg or two. Goodness knows, someone should."

Edward smiled at Longworth's bantering tone, but shook his head regretfully. "I fear we shall have to play another day, gentlemen. I need speak with you both."

Longworth sobered as soon as he saw the expression on Kingsley's face. Beside him, Marwood went very still. "What has happened?"

Edward's eyes flickered around the room. "Not here. Your house in twenty minutes, Lord Marwood."

Nothing more was said. Edward turned and left at once, Marwood and Longworth shortly thereafter. Marwood tried not to think about the grimness he had glimpsed in Edward's eyes, tried not to remember that it was the same grimness he'd seen in Longworth's just before he had set off for France.

Shortly gone half-past eleven, the three men stood assembled in Marwood's library. "All right, what's this all about?" Marwood asked without preamble.

Edward sighed. "It's not good, I am afraid." He paused, and glanced briefly at Longworth. "The French are on to Lavinia."

Longworth closed his eyes, clenching his fists tightly at his side. "How did they find her?"

"Osborne isn't sure. The details are sketchy at best, but it sounds as if she may have been spotted in a small village near Montcornet. Thankfully, Lavinia must have realized it herself. By the time the French arrived, she was already gone."

"Gone! But where *can* she go?" Longworth muttered.

"Osborne thinks she'll probably head for the coast."

Marwood drummed his fingers on the desk. "How is she travelling?"

"On horseback, I should imagine."

Longworth blanched. "She can't make it all the way from Montcornet to the coast on the back of a bloody horse!"

Edward glanced at Marwood. "No, she can't, which is why Osborne contacted me. One of us has to go to France and get her out."

Longworth stepped forward immediately. "There isn't any choice to be made. I'll go. This is a personal matter."

"I'm sorry, Nicholas, but you can't," Edward informed him sadly. "Neither you nor I can. Osborne has expressly forbidden it."

"Forbidden it! But he can't." Longworth was outraged. "We're talking about Lavinia's life here!"

"Which is exactly why you cannot go," Marwood spoke up quietly. "You and Edward were lucky to have escaped with your lives the last time, my friend. I doubt you would be so fortunate again."

"I fear you are right, Lord Marwood," Edward agreed. "The orders now would be to shoot on sight."

Marwood gazed at Edward with sudden comprehension. "That's why Osborne contacted you, wasn't it? To tell the three of us together why it had to be me."

Edward's sigh conveyed a certain heaviness of heart. "I wish I could say it were otherwise, my lord."

Marwood shook his head. "You don't have to. When you think about it, it only makes sense that I go. Lavinia knows me and I know her, so we won't have to waste time establishing identities. And I'm not under the same suspicion as the two of you." He drew himself up and glanced at Edward. "When does Osborne want me to set off?"

"He's expecting you at Whitehall within the hour. You probably leave tonight."

Longworth's hand trapped Marwood's arm in an iron grip. His voice was hoarse. "Devon, for God's sake, let me go with you. If anything were to happen—"

Marwood shook his head regretfully. "I can't, Nicholas. The French will have men everywhere—you know that. They would recognize you in an instant."

Longworth hung his head, forced to accept the truth of Marwood's statement. But it did not make him happy. "Let me take you as far as the coast," he said gruffly. "At least let me do that much."

Marwood nodded. He knew how hard this was for Longworth. "I'll bring her back, Nicholas. I promise."

Edward cleared his throat. "What are you going to tell Charlotte?"

Marwood kept his face expressionless. "I am not going to tell her anything," he said quietly. "If everything works out and I manage to come back with Lavinia, there will be no need for her to know that I was gone. She was worried enough about you, Edward. She doesn't need to go through it all again because of me. But there is something I think it only fair to tell you." He hesitated, and then quickly made up his mind. "Charlotte and I are no longer betrothed."

Edward was stunned. "Not betrothed? What are you talking about? Charlotte has said nothing of this to me."

"No, she hasn't. Because she didn't want you to know. Charlotte was concerned that your homecoming not be overshadowed by news of our own strife. We have also been keeping it to ourselves in an attempt not to overset Miss Harper."

"But what happened?"

Marwood shook his head. "It really doesn't matter anymore; the damage has long since been done. Suffice it to say that Charlotte was not to blame."

Edward nodded, his eyes fixed keenly on Marwood's face. "Do you still love her?"

"I never stopped loving her," Marwood said without hesitation. "It was my own stupidity which started this sorry state of affairs and my own jealousy which perpetuated it. As I said, Charlotte is not in any way responsible. However, I leave the decision whether she tells you the whole of the matter up to her."

Edward sighed, and stared at the man in front of him sadly. "I confess, Lord Marwood, I find it difficult to believe what you are telling me. I think I know my sister well, and I would be willing to wager a plum that she is still very much in love with you."

"Love is not the issue here, Edward, trust is. A trust which I violated, and which I am violating even now by telling you this. Charlotte was most adamant that you know nothing of what had gone on between us." Marwood glanced at him ruefully. "The only reason I am telling you now is because of the mission. At least if I do not come back, you will have heard the truth from my own lips."

Edward breathed a heavy sigh. "I appreciate your candour, Lord Marwood. And I am heartily sorry. This, coming on top of everything else, cannot be easy for you."

Marwood shrugged. "Perhaps my going to France will be good for everyone. It will give Charlotte some time on her own. I had intended to stop by your house and pay my respects to Miss Harper, anyway. I shall take the opportunity to speak briefly to Charlotte before I leave." He stared into the fire thoughtfully. "At least I will have had the chance to say goodbye."

MARWOOD MET with Osborne within the hour and, as expected, was to leave that night. A boat had already been secured to take him across the Channel. From there, he would be on his own.

Marwood did not linger on the thought of what lay ahead. It had never been his way. Dwelling on the possibility of what might happen was far too self-destructive. Better to deal with the problems as they arose. He knew there would be dangers, and he knew there was a very good chance that he or Lady Duplesse might not make it back. But that did not stop him from going ahead with the mission.

When Marwood arrived at Green Street, he was shown into the parlour where Charlotte and Edward reposed in matching wing-backed chairs on either side of the fireplace. They both looked up at his entrance.

Edward rose immediately. "Marwood, how are you?"

"Well, thank you, Kingsley, though I apologize for calling round so late." He glanced at Charlotte briefly. "I was occupied longer than I expected to be this afternoon."

"No need to apologize. We were just going in to dinner. Will you stay and join us?"

Marwood knew what Edward was asking. "No, I have plans for the evening," he said quietly. "But thank you for the offer. I just stopped by to pay my respects to Miss Harper.''

Edward nodded. From the expression on his face, it was evident that he was not surprised. He looked at Charlotte, then back towards Devon. "Right, then I shall take you up. Charlotte, are you coming?''

Charlotte shook her head. The sight of Devon standing there had caused her such intense pain, that it was like throwing salt in an open wound. "No, thank you, Edward, I think I will stay here.''

Marwood's voice was soft. "Surely your aunt will want to see the two of us together.''

"I have just been to see my aunt, Lord Marwood, and found her very well," Charlotte lied. "I advised her a few days ago that you might be coming to see her and that if you did, I would leave the two of you to visit in peace.''

Marwood stared down at her and sighed. What would Charlotte say if she knew he was going away on a dangerous assignment? Would she suddenly look at him through the eyes of love? Would she run into his arms and beg him to stay?

He had no way of knowing. Because he had no intention of changing his mind and telling her. He would not use his mission to France as an excuse to try to jolt Charlotte out of her apathy. If she did not come to him of her own volition, there was no point in her coming to him at all.

"Very well," Marwood said at last. "But I hope that I may speak with you when I come down.''

Charlotte said quietly. "I will be here, Lord Marwood.''

Marwood executed a brief, formal bow and then turned to follow Edward upstairs. Once he was gone,

Charlotte all but collapsed, her composure deserting her.

She had not expected to see Devon again so soon. The memory of the kiss she had witnessed between him and Lady Howard in the Park that morning had kept playing itself over and over in her mind like a horrible dream. She had wanted so much to prove Lady Howard wrong. She had prayed that the letter had been nothing more than a hoax, and that the rumours surrounding Lady Howard and her paramour were all lies.

But they were not. Charlotte could not deny what her eyes had seen, any more than she could ignore Lady Howard's warnings. It was clear that Devon had taken up with his old mistress again, and it was only a matter of time before Society knew.

Rising, Charlotte paced restlessly back and forth, her soft slippers making no sound on the pale green Aubusson carpet. She had purposely kept to her room since returning from Hyde Park, knowing that she would not be able to face anyone until she had been able to control her emotions. And for the most part, she had. She was no longer shocked, or angry, or even surprised. Over the hours, the violence of her emotions had faded into one dreadful ache. But that did not make seeing him now any easier.

A sound in the hall moments later brought Charlotte quickly around. She paled, her eyes widening in dismay at the sight of Marwood standing alone in the doorway. "Where is Edward?"

"He stayed to speak with Miss Harper for a bit." Marwood walked forward, unaware of her agitation. "Your aunt seems much improved."

Charlotte moistened her lower lip. "Yes, she has . . . resorted to her own medicines again." She paused, and glanced up at him thoughtfully. "Is it my imagination, or have you and Edward become quite close?"

"Your brother is a fine man, Charlotte. It is easy to see why you are so proud of him."

Charlotte lifted her chin. "He is an honourable man, above all."

Marwood detected the censorious note in her voice. "Are you saying that I am not?"

"I am not saying anything, my lord, but after what I learned today, I think it would be better if we were to tell everyone the truth of our relationship as quickly as possible."

Marwood hesitated. "What is it that you have learned?"

"That history has an unfortunate habit of repeating itself."

The earl's eyes glittered dangerously. "History?"

"Yes. Your... involvement with Lady Howard."

Marwood closed his eyes in exasperation. "Charlotte, must you keep bringing that up? It was a long time ago—"

"Then you *did* have a liaison with her," Charlotte shot back.

"Yes, all right, I admit it," Marwood shouted, goaded in spite of himself into response. "I was involved with Celia in the past, but—"

"And you are involved with her again!"

Marwood stared at her. "What do you mean?"

"Pray do not take me for a fool, Lord Marwood," Charlotte replied, her resolve strengthened by his audacious denial. "No wonder you told my brother you would be late. After what I saw in the Park this morning—"

"This morning!" Marwood repeated blankly. "What exactly did you see this morning?"

Charlotte's face glowed, and she hastily turned away.

"Oh, come, Charlotte, now is hardly the time to play the innocent. If you did not intend to divulge details, you should not have brought the subject up," Marwood said harshly. "Or am I supposed to guess what all this is about?"

"Spare me your sarcasm, Lord Marwood," Charlotte said tersely. "You know very well that I saw you kissing Lady Howard this morning."

Marwood slowly walked back towards her, his eyes boring into hers. "I don't know what you are talking about, Charlotte. I was neither in the Park, nor anywhere near Lady Howard this morning."

"Please do not lie to me, Lord Marwood! I saw the two of you together," she told him angrily.

"I don't know who or what you thought you saw, Charlotte, but it certainly wasn't me. And why should it bother you even if it was?" Devon retaliated. "You've already told me that there is nothing between us. If you don't care for me, why are you so concerned about my seeing another woman? If I didn't know better, I would swear you were still in love with me!"

Charlotte hastily turned away, but not before he had caught a glimpse of the anguish in her eyes.

"That's it, isn't it, Charlotte. You do still love me."

Charlotte drew in a sharp breath and whirled round, anger and dismay reflected in her clear blue eyes. "You must be mad!" she whispered. "I could no more love you than I could—could—"

"Than you could what, Charlotte?" Marwood taunted her, stepping closer. "Than you could hate me?"

"No, I—"

"Go on, say it, Charlotte," Marwood urged, gripping her by the shoulders and pulling her towards him. "You could no more love me than you could hate me!"

Charlotte gasped at the hard strength of his fingers. "Lord Marwood!" she began, outraged. "How dare—"

"No, don't even begin to dare me, Charlotte," Marwood whispered silkily. His dark eyes peered into hers with an intensity that frightened her. "You still love me. If you did not, you wouldn't be so upset at the thought of my being involved with another woman. Just as I was half out of my mind with jealousy over the thought of you being with another man!"

"It is not the same!" Charlotte shouted at him.

"It *is* the same, because you know damn well there's no truth to this senseless accusation of yours with regard to myself and Lady Howard!"

"It is true!" Charlotte closed her eyes. "She told me herself that you and I weren't happy. She knew we had broken off our betrothal. How would she know that unless you told her! And what about the letter telling me that the two of you were going to meet in the Park? You even told my brother that you were going to be late meeting him!"

"Yes, I did. Because I had forgotten when I made the appointment with Edward that I was already scheduled to see my solicitor. That was why I had to delay our bout. But as far as the rest of it goes, I haven't a clue what you're talking about. In fact, it seems to me that someone has gone to a great deal of trouble to make you think that Lady Howard and I are involved again, and judging by your reaction—" his voice softened slightly

"—the thought of that happening causes you a great deal of distress."

Charlotte tilted her chin. "It causes me no distress at all—"

"You're lying." Devon's words cut right across her denial. "You are unhappy about it, and there's only one reason why you would be. You still love me. Do you, Charlotte?" Marwood growled throatily. "Do you still love me?"

It would have been so easy to say yes, Charlotte admitted. To say yes and then just fall blindly into the warmth of his arms. To forget all about her pride and the humiliation this man had caused her. Here, now, with that beloved face so close, it would have been so easy to say the one word which held them apart, to turn her back on her pride and go to him again.

Yet, even as her body longed for him, Charlotte knew that she could not do it. Devon had doubted her once; there was absolutely no reason to think that he would not do so again.

About to fling the angry words back in his face, Charlotte gasped as Devon gave a sudden, unexpected groan and pulled her into his arms, silencing her protest with the heat of his mouth. She felt the unexpected fire of his hands caressing her shoulders, his fingers burning into her skin like a red-hot iron. She trembled, and wrenched her mouth from his. "Devon! Stop!"

Capturing her parted lips under his own, Devon kissed her again with an intimacy that fanned the slumbering flames of desire into a raging fire. She felt the traitorous response of her own body as Devon ran the softness of his tongue along her lips, slipping inside to taste the sweetness within. Her breath caught in her throat as she felt his hand at her dress, easing the tiny puff sleeve off her left shoulder to expose the exquisite perfection of one smoothly rounded breast. She felt the touch of his mouth searing her skin, the rough caress of his chin inflaming her senses. "Devon!"

"Tell me you don't want me now, Charlotte," he murmured, pressing his lips against the wildly beating pulse at her throat. "Tell me you don't want me to love you."

Charlotte felt herself being lowered down onto the settee. She felt his weight on top of her, pressing intimately against her until she was filled a longing she could not even begin to put a name to. A deep, dark longing which cried out to be answered.

"Tell me you want me, Charlotte," Devon breathed softly against her breast. "Tell me!"

Charlotte arched to his touch, aware that her body was telling him what her words did not. The musky, masculine scent of him filled her nostrils, blinding her to everything but her need, her desire for this man.

"I love you, Charlotte," Marwood whispered softly, his voice rough with passion. "More than I thought possible. You fill my mind until I cannot see straight."

Charlotte shook her head, struggling to regain control of her emotions. "No, this is wrong!" she cried, fighting to pull herself out of his arms, away from the chaos of emotions his touch had provoked. "You do not . . . love me!" she gasped as his hand reached out to caress her again. "And I will not be . . . used again!"

It was the anguish in her voice which finally pierced Marwood's driving passion, and her anger which caused him to stop. "Used?"

Marwood rose from the settee in one lithe movement. "Is that what you consider I have done, Charlotte? Used you?"

Charlotte swallowed, and pushed herself upright, unsteadily pulling the fabric of her gown back onto her shoulder. "What would you have me call it, sir? You are obviously using our mock betrothal as a cover-up for the relationship which now exists between yourself and Lady Howard. She has already told me—"

"I will listen to no more," he interrupted, in a voice she scarcely recognized. "I have humbled myself at your feet twice, and I shall not do so again. I have told you that I love you, and have apologized more than once for my lack of trust. I have been willing to perpetrate the charade that is our betrothal for the sake of your family and friends. And I have sworn to you on my honour that I am not involved with Lady Howard. Yet, in spite of everything, you still choose to disbelieve me. So be it."

Marwood walked towards the door. "I will not trouble you again, Miss Kingsley, nor will you be called upon to act the part of my fiancée. I had hoped that I might leave here tonight under considerably different circumstances, but I see that such is not possible. Too wide a chasm separates us now. One which I fear neither of us will ever be able to cross. And for that I am truly sorry. Goodbye, Charlotte!"

And then, he was gone, the door closing with an unmistakably final click behind him.

CHAPTER ELEVEN

LONGWORTH'S CARRIAGE made good time to the coast
The horses were fresh, and the road was clearly illumi
nated by the silvery light of the moon.

The two men had not spoken a great deal since set
ting off from London. Cognizant of the gravity of the
mission, as well as of the dangers inherent with it, they
both understood that there was a good chance the mis
sion might fail. But as he studied his friend's averted
face in the semi-darkness of the carriage, Longworth
suspected that Marwood's silence stemmed more from
his recent meeting with Charlotte than it did from any
thing else.

"Rough parting?" he enquired now.

Marwood looked out through the carriage window
his gaze focussed somewhere on the moonlit fields be
yond. The anger he had felt at Charlotte's rejection wa
already gone only to leave an unbearable ache. "I vouch
walking into a lion's den would have garnered me a les
savage raking than the one I received at Charlotte'
hands tonight."

Softly spoken as they were, there was no mistaking
the pain behind the words. "What happened?" Long
worth asked.

Marwood sighed. "Quite apart from the fact that
behaved like an unprincipled boor, Charlotte is pos
sessed of the singularly ridiculous notion that I an

somehow involved with Celia again.'' The earl's voice was distant. ''Says she saw me kissing her in the Park the other morning. At dawn, no less.''

''Kissing her!'' Longworth stared, thunderstruck. ''Where the devil would she get an idea like that?''

''I have no idea, and I was too bloody angry at the time to ask.''

''Well, you will simply have to enquire when you get back.''

Marwood glanced at him cryptically. ''Yes, I shall do that.''

They subsided into silence. A few minutes later, Longworth said abruptly, ''I say, what was Miss Kingsley doing in the Park at dawn, anyway? Dashed uncivilized time for a lady to be abroad.''

Marwood shook his head. ''Damned if I know. What does anyone do in Hyde Park at that time of the day which isn't illegal, immoral or illicit?''

''Nothing else I can think of,'' Longworth replied, ''which probably means that Celia was meeting a lover. But that doesn't explain why Miss Kingsley was there. She's not the type to trouble herself with other people's liaisons.''

''No, she isn't. Unless—'' Marwood drew himself up in the seat, suddenly remembering Charlotte's brief mention of a letter. His eyes narrowed thoughtfully. ''Unless she was led to believe that the man in the Park that morning would be me.''

''You!'' Longworth cocked an eyebrow. ''Why would she think it was you? More important, who would want to give her such an impression?''

''Someone who might like to drive a wedge between Charlotte and myself.'' Marwood glanced at his friend

shrewdly. "Think about it, Nicholas. Who would enjoy seeing my betrothal to Charlotte come to an end?"

"Apart from Celia herself, I can't think of anyone
who—" Nicholas abruptly broke off, his eyes widening. "Good Lord, Celia?"

Marwood spread his hands. "Why not? She's made
no secret of the fact that she would welcome me back in
her bed. Either that or she wants to get back at me for
my having rejected her."

"Revenge?" Longworth's brows drew together. "I
say, that's an interesting notion. Come to think of it,
Celia has been in a devil of a pucker since you broke off
your liaison. Still, I didn't think she would stoop this
low."

Marwood smiled sardonically. "You know what they
say about a woman spurned."

"Hmm, I am beginning to think they were right,"
Longworth acknowledged ruefully. "Must remember
never to get Lavinia jealous. It does seem rather strange,
though, Celia trying to break up an engaged couple."

"Maybe she didn't think it would be all that difficult
a thing to do," Marwood replied. "Maybe she already
knew that Charlotte and I were having problems."

"Eh? But how?"

"Unless Charlotte said something, which I doubt, I
can only assume that Celia overheard you and I talking
at Lady Wilton's soirée. I grant you, Charlotte's behaviour has been less than warm upon occasion, but it
has certainly not been cool enough to warrant anyone's
assuming we were no longer betrothed. Celia must have
known that something was wrong."

"That would also explain Celia's so-called charitable visit to Miss Harper. You yourself intimated that

there was probably another reason for her being at Charlotte's house."

"Yes, I do, and now that you mention it, it was shortly after Celia's visit that Charlotte began to distance herself from me again." Marwood's eyes darkened fiercely. "I'll wager Celia dropped a number of not-so-subtle remarks before she left."

Longworth nodded. "It would explain a lot, my friend. So, what do you intend to do about it?"

Marwood was silent for a moment. "There's not very much I can do at the moment. Finding Lavinia and getting her safely out of France is my main concern right now, and will occupy all of my time over the next little while. But you can be sure of one thing. Something will be done immediately upon my return." Marwood's voice dropped to a whisper. "I told Charlotte it was over between us tonight, that I was tired of having to vindicate myself in her eyes. But now I'm beginning to understand why she has been acting the way she has. Celia has been putting doubts into her mind. And to that end, I intend to pay a visit to Lady Howard as soon as I get back. She has some explaining to do, and I *will* have the truth from her." Marwood's face darkened menacingly. "If I discover that Celia has been meddling in my affairs, she is going to be very sorry, indeed!"

SOMEHOW, CHARLOTTE managed not to lose her mind over the next few days. She went to bed early and rose late, leaving word with Dickens that she was not at home to anyone who called. She endeavoured to occupy her mind with books, but found she could not concentrate. She took up her needlepoint and promptly pricked her finger. Everything she touched seemed to fall apart, a sad reminder that her life was doing exactly the same.

Edward watched his sister go about her daily routine, drifting from room to room as silently as a ghost, and forced himself not to interfere. How could he, when he had no way of knowing whether Marwood had changed his mind and told Lotte that he was leaving for France, or whether his sister's preoccupation was of a more personal nature. Until Charlotte chose to tell him the truth of the matter himself, he could say nothing. After all, he had given Marwood his word.

By the evening of the fifth day, however, Edward knew that he could no longer hold his silence. Charlotte was heading into a decline. She did little more than pick at her food and had taken to avoiding most social functions. And while he had initially been torn between his loyalty to Marwood and his devotion to Charlotte, there was really no question which was the stronger force. His sister's health came first.

He waited until they had retired to the drawing-room before gently launching into his assault.

"So, Lotte," he began after Dickens set the tea tray next to Charlotte. "Would you care to tell me what happened between you and Devon last week? And please do not try to pretend that you don't know what I am talking about."

Charlotte poured milk into her brother's cup and did exactly that. "In truth, Edward, I cannot think what you refer to."

"I refer, Lotte, to the fact that you haven't been yourself since the day Lord Marwood left. You're not eating, you don't go out, and I never see you smile anymore." He watched her carefully, trying to gauge her reaction. "Did Lord Marwood say anything to overset you before he left?"

"No!"

The word sounded loud, even to Charlotte's ears, and she quickly picked up the teapot, purposely avoiding her brother's questioning gaze. He had always been able to see far too much when he looked directly into her eyes. "Why would you ask?" she eventually continued in a more rational tone.

"No reason. But does it not strike you strange that he has not called round this week?"

"I assume he has been busy with other matters."

"I see. And you're sure the two of you did not quarrel?"

"Quarrel? Of course not, Edward." Charlotte quickly put the pot down again, afraid that he might notice how badly her hands were shaking. "Why would you think such a thing? In fact, why are you asking me all these questions? It is not like you to pry."

Edward put down his cup. "Because I was not being completely honest just now, Lotte. I was trying to find out exactly what was bothering you."

"But why?"

"Because I know that you have, in fact, ended your betrothal to Lord Marwood."

Charlotte stared at her brother in shock. "How did you know that?" Her brows drew together in dismay. "Did Laura tell you?"

"No, Laura has said nothing." Edward hesitated. Then, plunging ahead he said, "Marwood told me himself. He thought it wise ... under the circumstances."

"He had no right to tell you, Edward. We agreed that—" She halted abruptly. "What circumstances?"

"The circumstances that he...might not come back."

"Not come back?" Charlotte shook her head in confusion. "What are you talking about, Edward, why would he not come back? Where has he gone?"

There was a slight pause. "He didn't tell you, then."

It was not really a question, and Charlotte felt her heart turn over. "Tell me what?"

Edward rose and walked towards the window. "I don't know that I have the right to tell you, Lotte. Obviously, Marwood did not want you to know."

"Know what?" Charlotte got to her feet and followed him. "Edward, tell me. What did Devon not want me to know?"

Edward turned round and gazed into his sister's face. There was no mistaking the fear he saw there. "Marwood has gone to France," he told her softly. "He left right after seeing you the other night."

"*What?*"

Edward heard the panic in his sister's voice but knew it was too late to stop now. She had to be told. "Lord Longworth was waiting to take him to the coast. From there, Marwood was to board a ship bound for Calais."

"Calais? But why? What manner of personal business could Devon have in France?"

"None. He has gone under orders from Lord Osborne."

Charlotte stared at her brother in disbelief. "But I thought Lord Osborne was *your* commanding officer. He came here to see you. He never mentioned anything about Devon."

Edward smiled sadly. "He would have no reason to, Lotte. Osborne is hardly going to disclose the names of his agents, even to the sister of one of them. You wouldn't have known Longworth was involved if it hadn't been for our own close association.''

"Good Lord.'' Charlotte fixed him with a wide-eyed stare. "Are you telling me that all three of you were... that is, are...*spies* for the Crown?''

Edward nodded. "Longworth and I are still on active service. Marwood retired when he succeeded to the title.''

"But I don't understand,'' Charlotte said weakly. "If Devon was retired, why did he go to France now? Why did Lord Osborne call him back?''

"To carry out a mission neither Longworth nor myself could undertake. Osborne refused to allow either of us to go back into France. He knew it would be too dangerous.''

"But why Devon?'' Charlotte repeated, her voice an anguished murmur. "Surely there was someone else who could have gone?''

Her brother shook his head. "No one of Marwood's calibre, I'm afraid, and this mission was far too dangerous to entrust to just anyone. Too much is at stake.''

Charlotte was seized by a chill of apprehension. "What exactly has Devon gone to do?''

"To rescue an agent we have been trying to get out of France for some time now. A lady who is in very great danger of losing her life.''

"A lady? Dear God!'' Charlotte whispered. "Edward, please, for pity's sake, tell me what is going on.''

"Sit down, Charlotte.'' Edward took a deep breath. "I fear this is not going to be an easy story to tell.''

And it wasn't. By the time Edward finished, Charlotte's head was spinning.

"But why did he not tell me?" Charlotte uttered in a strangled voice. "We had that silly fight—we both said things we shouldn't. What if he doesn't come back?"

"He knew the risks before he accepted the mission, Charlotte. And the reason he did not tell you was because he loved you. He didn't want you to worry."

Charlotte tensed, her eyes lifting to his face. "He said that?"

"Yes. Just after he told me that you were no longer betrothed and that it was as a result of something he had done."

Charlotte winced. "Did he tell you what it was?"

"No. He left the decision to tell me up to you. He did say, however, that it had something to do with trust and that you were not in any way responsible."

A wave of guilt washed over Charlotte and she closed her eyes, choking back a sob. "He didn't tell you the truth, Edward. He should have told you that I was just as much to blame. Maybe more. I wouldn't forgive him. He tried to apologize, but I was too proud to listen. Oh, Teddy, what am I going to do?" Charlotte hastily blinked back tears. "When I think of what I said to him before he left . . . what I accused him of . . ."

Edward slanted her a wary glance. "You accused him of something?"

Charlotte clasped her hands together in her lap, aware that they were trembling badly. "I thought that he and Lady Howard were . . . having an affair."

"An affair! With Lady Howard? Good Lord, Lotte." Edward was clearly taken aback by the remark. "Whatever would have made you think such a thing? Marwood is an honourable gentleman. He would never conduct himself in such a manner."

"I hadn't thought he would, but after everything Lady Howard told me, I began to wonder. And then when I received the letter—"

"A letter?" Edward glanced at her sharply. "From whom?"

"I don't know. There was no signature."

"Was it from a man or a woman?"

"I don't know," Charlotte repeated numbly. "It was...printed in block letters. I could not tell."

"What did it say?"

"It insinuated that Devon would meet a lady in the Park at dawn. That it was—" Charlotte's gaze slid away from his "—a lovers' meeting."

"And you believed it?"

"I saw no reason not to," Charlotte shot back, hurt. "Lady Howard had made no secret of the fact that she wanted Devon back. She even went so far as to tell me that he already had come back to her, and that since our betrothal was at an end, I might as well let him go. How could she have known that Devon and I were no longer affianced if Devon didn't tell her?"

"I don't know." Edward's eyes narrowed. "What about this letter? Did you go to the Park?"

Charlotte veiled her eyes with her lashes. "Yes."

"And did you see Lady Howard with Marwood?"

"Yes."

Edward leaned forward. "Are you *sure* it was Marwood?"

"I did not see his face," Charlotte admitted, "but it looked exactly like him. He was wearing Devon's black coat, and riding a black stallion just like Emperor. Who else could it have been?"

"Any number of gentlemen, I should think," Edward muttered. "Lady Howard is a very devious woman, Charlotte, and a jealous one. If, as you say, she knew that you and Marwood were having problems, she wouldn't think twice about using that information to her own advantage. No doubt she set up the rendezvous to look like a lovers' tryst and then sent you an anonymous letter to make sure you would be there to witness it. I'd venture to say the gentleman with her in the Park that morning knew about the subterfuge and was a party to it.''

Charlotte sat up. ''Then the letter *was* a hoax.''

''I am inclined to think so,'' Edward said, ''though Lady Howard is not likely to admit it. For that reason, I think you had best make it very clear the next time you see her that you and Marwood are still very much betrothed. It may just provoke her into saying something out of hand.''

Charlotte nodded, her eyes darkening with anger. ''I suspect the opportunity will present itself at Lady Rowallayne's ball tomorrow evening. I am sure Lady Howard will be attending, and so shall we.'' She glanced at her brother quickly. ''I hope you have not forgotten your promise to accompany me, Teddy.''

''I hadn't forgotten, nor am I about to renege on my commitment,'' Edward told her drily. ''I may need to be there to stop you and Lady Howard coming to blows!''

LADY ROWALLAYNE'S ballroom was a glittering mass of silks and taffetas by the time Charlotte and Edward arrived. People were standing and chatting in every corner of the room and overflowing onto the balcony through the open French doors. The air was scented with the delicate fragrance of the ladies' perfumes and the sweet smell of flowers—thousands of them were banked along the length of the room and set in bunches throughout the antechambers.

At the entrance to the ballroom, Charlotte paused to gaze out over the huge crowd. She looked stunning in a gown of ice blue silk over an underslip of silver lace, with tiny puffed sleeves embroidered with fine silver thread. Her dark hair was arranged in an elegant cluster of curls drawn high atop her head and held in place by two diamond clips. Her lovely features were pale but composed, thanks to Edward's presence beside her.

It had taken Charlotte a long time to come to terms with the knowledge that Devon might not return from France. While Edward had related the details as briefly and as painlessly as possible, there was no disguising the fact that the assignment was extremely dangerous.

It was the threat to Devon's life which had succeeded in stripping away all Charlotte's doubts and insecurities, finally forcing her to admit that it was her own stubborn pride which had prevented her from forgiving him; the same stubbornness which had not allowed her to see that jealousy had caused Devon to misinterpret Edward's letter.

Edward felt the unconscious pressure of Charlotte's fingers on his arm and looked at her, sensing her anxiety. "Lotte, are you going to be all right?"

Charlotte took a deep breath, and then nodded. Her mouth was dry, her lips curved in a stiff smile. "I shall be fine, Teddy. I am just so very afraid for him."

Her voice broke unexpectedly, and Edward put his hand over hers in a reassuring gesture. "He'll be fine, Lotte, trust me. Marwood is one of the best. Osborne wouldn't have sent him to do the job if he hadn't thought he could handle it. Besides," he added with a brief laugh, "there is more than just England's safety at stake here. I understand Marwood undertook this as a personal favour to Longworth."

Charlotte looked up at him in surprise. "But what has this to do with Lord Longworth?"

"A great deal, when you consider that Nicholas is very much in love with the lady Devon has gone to rescue. Right," Edward said, bracing himself. "Let's get on with this, shall we?"

Arm in arm, Edward and Charlotte descended the long staircase and made their way into the crowded room, nodding and smiling at acquaintances. As it was Edward's first really large Society gathering, it was hardly surprising that he attracted attention, particularly the attention of those matchmaking matrons with marriageable daughters. The advent of any good-looking, eligible gentleman would garner notice; the fact that Edward was a hero only added to his cachet.

It soon became clear, however, that Edward's attention was already fixed on one particular young lady, and as soon as Charlotte spotted Laura chatting with Lord Dreighton, they made directly for her side.

Charlotte forced a gaiety into her tone she was far from feeling. "Good evening, Laura, Lord Dreighton."

Laura turned towards the newcomers, her own face brightening. "Oh, Charlotte, how very pleased I am to see you. And Mr. Kingsley. I thought after the other afternoon you might have decided to avoid Society altogether."

"The idea had crossed my mind, but I did promise Charlotte that I would escort her this evening." Edward smiled a greeting to the other man. "How are you, Lord Dreighton?"

"Can't complain, Kingsley, can't complain. Good to see you home again. And Miss Kingsley, may I say that you are looking quite the thing. Where is your handsome fiancé this evening?"

Charlotte faltered, leaving Edward to step in. "I fear Lord Marwood had to head up to the country for a bit, Lord Dreighton. Matters concerning the estate."

"Dear me, that little problem again. Pity he doesn't get a decent steward up there to manage things. Would save him all this dashed running back and forth."

"Save who all this running back and forth, Lord Dreighton?" Lady Howard said, gliding up to their group.

Charlotte tensed at the sound of the silky, feminine voice, and steeled herself for the confrontation. She had known it was only a matter of time before Lady Howard sought her out. Feeling that she had wounded her prey, Lady Howard was no doubt intending to close in for the kill. Little did she know, that the tables had abruptly been turned.

Charlotte smiled politely. "We were talking about my fiancé, Lady Howard."

"Really." Celia glanced around the room with interest. "And where is the dashing earl this evening, Miss Kingsley? Surely you have not come without him yet again?"

Charlotte flushed, but refused to be drawn. "Unfortunately, Lord Marwood was called away to attend to some problems in the country, which is why Lord Dreighton was commenting that he required a good steward."

"I see. How convenient." Celia turned to regard the elderly peer, and laughed mockingly. "Does it not strike you a little strange, Lord Dreighton, that Miss Kingsley is more often without her fiancé than with him?''

Lord Dreighton looked thoughtful. "Can't say that it surprises me unduly, Lady Howard. The earl's a busy man. Probably hasn't much time for all these Society gatherings."

Lady Howard's smile flashed thinly. "No, perhaps he hasn't. As you say, always busy doing one thing . . . or another."

Charlotte stiffened. Beside her, Edward smiled laconically. "Speaking of absent loved ones, where is Lord Howard this evening, Lady Howard? Is he perhaps indisposed?"

Celia's smile did not quite reach her cold green eyes. "On the contrary, Mr. Kingsley, my husband's health is excellent. He is simply not a devotee of affairs of this nature, and as I am just as happy to attend on my own, it makes for a mutually satisfactory arrangement."

"Well, I'm sure you do not lack for company at any of these . . . affairs, Lady Howard," Charlotte said bluntly.

Celia flushed unbecomingly. "I would be careful about your comments, Miss Kingsley. I thought, perhaps, that there might be another reason for Lord Marwood's absence this evening, *if* you take my meaning."

Mindful of Edward's eyes upon on her, Charlotte replied with admirable poise, "I cannot imagine why you would think so, Lady Howard. If Lord Marwood were in London, he would certainly be with me. My fiancé and I are eager to spend as much time together as possible, especially now that the date for the wedding has been established."

Charlotte was pleased to see Lady Howard's composure slip. "You have . . . set the date?"

"Yes. Devon and I discussed it before he left for the country. We both decided that there was no point in waiting any longer. As you can imagine, I await his return with great pleasure."

Lady Howard's countenance darkened. "Yes, I am sure you do." She glanced at Edward suspiciously. "And are you also happy the date has been set, Mr. Kingsley?"

Edward's reply was as smooth as glass. "I await the day with great impatience, Lady Howard. I'm sure you can imagine how delighted I am with the match. I told Lord Marwood as much before he left."

"You told him that?" Celia turned an unbecoming shade of grey. "Excuse me."

Lord Dreighton watched her go. "Lady Howard seems a trifle out of curl this evening, don't you think, Miss Kingsley?"

Charlotte opened her fan. "I cannot say that I noticed, Lord Dreighton. Did you, Edward?"

Edward shook his head and smiled down at her proudly. "Can't say that I did, Lotte. Can't say that I did."

THE REST OF THE EVENING seemed interminable. Charlotte danced, she chatted, she offered the appropriate responses where required and tried to act as though her heart and her thoughts were not a hundred miles away in the French countryside.

Thankfully, Lady Howard did not resume her attack. Charlotte felt the daggers of the woman's glances a few times throughout the evening, but was not troubled by anything beyond that. No doubt the she-wolf was lying low, licking her wounds. She had not been able to inflict the injury she had intended to, and was now left to try to fathom exactly how things stood between the elusive Marwood and his fiancée.

Charlotte took care to maintain her appearance of tranquillity well into the evening. She did not display, by word or action, that Lady Howard's continued surveillance gave her the slightest cause for concern. She was growing more and more convinced that Edward had been right, that Lady Howard had been lying to her all along in an attempt to make her doubt Devon.

By midnight, however, the strain of the deception finally began to take its toll. She was having trouble concentrating, and more than once had to be recalled to attention. From across the room, Edward noticed his sister's increasing distraction and leisurely made his way to her side.

"Lotte," he said, casually drawing her aside, "you look about ready to scream."

"I'm afraid I shall if I have to answer one more question about Devon's whereabouts, and when we are to be married. I don't know that I can carry on much longer."

"Perhaps we should leave?"

Charlotte sighed. "I should dearly love to, but I fear it is a little early."

"I don't know why." Edward's gaze took in the drooping flowers and the long trails of wax on the candles. "Surely we have been here long enough to appease Society."

Charlotte smiled wistfully. "Society is a hard mistress, Edward. You must take pains to please her or she will come back at you in anger tenfold."

"Then why don't you slip upstairs for a few minutes," Edward suggested quietly. "I'm sure no one will notice your absence. Lord knows it would be impossible to tell who's here and who isn't. Besides, I haven't seen hide nor hair of Lady Howard in the past ten minutes, so she's not likely to miss you, either. Laura and I will make any excuses necessary."

"Laura?" In spite of her weariness, Charlotte couldn't resist giving her brother a teasing look. "Is that not being a little familiar, Teddy?"

"I meant Miss Beaufort, and never mind smiling at me like that, Lotte. It was an inadvertent slip."

Charlotte quickly bit back her retort. "Bless you, Teddy. I don't know what I would do without you. And yes, I think I could use a few minutes alone."

Taking a casual look round, Charlotte started towards the door, slipping out of the ballroom and making her way up the stairs. She decided against going to the ladies' withdrawing-room, fearing the possibility of running into Lady Howard, and turned left at the top of the stairs instead of right. She paused at the first door she came to.

Glancing down the length of the deserted hall, Charlotte leaned her ear against the door and then cautiously pushed it open. Fortunately, her stealth was not necessary. The music room was empty, its only occupants a beautifully lacquered harpsichord and a fine Welsh harp which stood on an elevated platform in front of the window.

Breathing a thankful sigh, Charlotte slipped inside and closed the door behind her. Abruptly, all sounds of the ball disappeared, leaving her in blessed silence. She was finally to be granted a few moments of peace.

The smile faded from her face as thoughts of Devon rushed back in, filling her mind with worry. Unanswered questions flew in and out like pigeons to a rookery. Had Devon found the lady he was seeking? Had they managed to get to the coast undetected. Where they still alive?

Did Devon still love her?

Charlotte closed her eyes and leaned her forehead against the edge of the harp. She had never suffered such uncertainty. She had to believe that Devon was safe. How could she go on if he were not? There was so much that had to be set right between them, so many words that needed to be said. He had to come back so that she could say them. He had to!

A gentle evening breeze suddenly stirred the curtains and wafted in through the open window. It teased the wispy tendrils of hair around Charlotte's face, cooling her overheated cheeks. It also blew in the conversation of the two people standing in the shadows of the balcony directly below.

"So, where is he tonight?" Charlotte heard a man say gruffly. "Do you think your plan has finally worked?"

The woman's laugh was uncertain. "I don't know. I thought it had when he didn't come in with Miss Kingsley, but now I am not so sure. It would appear that Marwood's absence stems from nothing more serious than a visit to the country."

Charlotte gasped, and then froze in shocked silence. Lady Howard and Lord Barrymore were below!

"What about Miss Kingsley?" Barrymore continued, completely unaware of Charlotte's presence above.

"I don't know. Either she's a very good actress, or I misjudged the situation. The little ninnyhammer took great delight in telling me that she and Marwood had set the date, and that she was missing him dreadfully."

Barrymore chuckled. "Sounds as if you may have been wasting your time, Celia. Perhaps the relationship wasn't as shaky as you thought."

"I know what I heard," Celia snapped. "That night at Lady Wilton's soirée, I distinctly heard Lord Longworth say that Charlotte had ended the betrothal. Why do you think I started this whole game in the first place?"

"Well, obviously your little ruse in Hyde Park didn't work," Barrymore observed cryptically. "Miss Kingsley would hardly be talking about wedding dates now if it had."

"I can't understand what went wrong. She must have believed the letter you sent. She was there. I saw her."

Charlotte heard the anger in Lady Howard's voice, but knew her words were laced with desperation. Barrymore, however, was obviously a good deal more complacent about the whole thing. "Perhaps she recognized me and realized it was a trick," he said.

"How could she have recognized you? I barely did, and I was standing right there!"

"Yes, you were, and I enjoyed that kiss very much." Barrymore's voice turned suddenly husky. "Speaking of which, when am I going to get the rest of my payment for helping you with this, my sweet Celia?"

Charlotte heard the sounds of a scuffle, and then a dull thud.

"Oof! What did you hit me for?" Barrymore groaned. "You didn't stop me the last time—"

"I fear I have changed my mind since the last time, Lord Barrymore." Lady Howard's voice was not in the least romantic. "It would seem that you are not as necessary as I had anticipated."

The bickering carried on, but Charlotte did not stop to listen. She had already heard all that she needed to. In one brief conversation, all her questions had been answered. "Forgive me, Devon, forgive me," Charlotte whispered fervently.

Abruptly, she turned and fled the music room. She had to get back to the ballroom. She had to find Edward as quickly as possible to tell him that Lady Howard had indeed been playing a devious game, and that he had been right in his suspicions. If only she had been as wise!

Fortunately, Charlotte did not have far to look. Edward was standing at the entrance to the grand ballroom, slightly apart from the crowd. In her excitement, she failed to notice the gentleman standing beside him.

"Edward, you will never guess what I have just heard. You were right about Lady—"

Charlotte's words came to an abrupt halt as she realized that Lord Longworth was standing with her brother. Her stomach knotted as she saw the expressions on both men's faces. "What has happened?"

Neither man spoke. "Edward, please tell me! Have you had some news? Is Devon back?"

Edward's eyes were dark with grief. "I'm sorry, Lotte, the news isn't good. Nicholas has just come from Lord Osborne."

His voice broke. Charlotte forced herself to ask the question. "And?"

"Apparently, the ship which was to have brought Devon and Lavinia back landed hours ago."

Was to have brought back? Charlotte fought to stem the rising tide of nausea. "And?"

Longworth shook his head sadly. "We don't know what happened, Miss Kingsley. Apparently, the captain waited as long as he could. Marwood and Lavinia . . . never made the rendezvous."

CHAPTER TWELVE

NEVER MADE THE RENDEZVOUS.

Charlotte sat up in bed, slowly sipping the strange tasting herbal tea Aunt Kittie had made for her, and tried not to hear the words which kept running round and round her head.

The captain waited as long as he could.

She remembered Nicholas Longworth's uttering those words as distinctly as though it were only last night. Except that it wasn't last night. It was more than two weeks ago. And in those two weeks there had been no news about Devon.

Charlotte took another sip of the lukewarm tea and stared into the darkened fireplace. She remembered little of what had happened after Longworth had spoken those fateful words. She knew that Edward had brought her home and that he had left again almost immediately. She knew that Anna had helped her to undress and that she had crawled into bed, numb with fear and shock. And she knew that, once started, the tears had not stopped falling until there were no more left to cry.

She had finally fallen into an exhausted sleep. The next morning she awoke, red-eyed and groggy, knowing that the pain of Devon's disappearance was still with her. Until he returned, it would remain with her.

EDWARD WAS already at the breakfast table when Charlotte finally came down. She was dressed in a becoming azure blue morning gown, its deep colour making her pale skin appear even more translucent so that her eyes seemed almost too large for her face. "Good morning, Teddy."

Edward started, and glanced up at her in surprise. "Lotte! I didn't even hear you come in. I swear, you're as bad as I am."

Charlotte smiled wanly, and signalled Dickens to bring a fresh pot of coffee. "Education by example, I suppose. Is Aunt Kittie down yet?"

"Mmm, I think I saw her heading towards the back kitchen about half an hour ago." Edward gave a short laugh. "Ever since Dr. Palfrey told her she could get up and start moving about, there's been no stopping her. In fact, I think she is trying to make up for lost time. She mentioned something about a tonic for Lady Bering. Said she wanted to see you after breakfast, if you haven't anything planned."

"I haven't." Charlotte helped herself to a small serving of toast and eggs from the well laden sideboard, not because she was hungry, but because she knew Edward would scold if she didn't. "I am so relieved that Aunt Kittie is feeling better."

"Yes, so are the ladies of the ton, I understand," Edward commented wryly. He shot Charlotte a concerned glance, trying not to be alarmed by the sight of the violet smudges beneath her eyes. "What about you, Lotte? Did you sleep any better last night?"

"Yes, much better, thank you, Teddy," Charlotte lied. She sat down across from him and shook out her napkin. "It must have been Aunt Kittie's tea. But tell

me, how was your drive with Laura yesterday afternoon? She did not say too much about it when I saw her
last evening.''

At the slow, tender smile which curved Edward's
mouth, Charlotte felt a momentary lessening of her own
unhappiness. "Oh, Teddy, I am glad. You're in love
with her, aren't you?''

Edward's smooth cheeks reddened. "That obvious,
is it?''

"Only to me." Charlotte's soft laughter flowed gently
across the space between them. "Your face gives you
away, I'm afraid. Are you going to marry her?''

"If she will have me." Edward glanced at his sister,
and then ruffled her hair fondly. "I never could fool
you, could I, poppet.''

"We could never fool one another," Charlotte cor-
rected him. She busied herself with buttering her toast.
"I have no doubt that my own emotions are...equally
apparent.''

Edward took a sip of his coffee, and studied his sister. "Charlotte, I hope you won't think I am prying,''
he began slowly, "but what started all this in the first
place? The mix up regarding your betrothal, I mean.
What exactly did Lord Marwood do that was so bad?''

Charlotte could not prevent the sudden surge of colour to her cheeks. "Oh, dear, I was afraid you were
going to ask that sooner or later. And you will probably laugh at me when I tell you, in light of everything
that has gone on with Lady Howard.'' Charlotte
paused, and took a deep breath. "Lord Marwood
thought I was...involved with another man.''

Edward gazed at his sister in astonishment. "I beg
your pardon. Did you say...another man?''

Charlotte smiled weakly. "He thought it was *you!*"

"Me?" Edward stared into her face. "*I* . . . was the other gentleman? Egad, Charlotte, I fear you have lost me this time. Would you care to explain what this is all about?"

The recounting of the story took a good deal of time, but Charlotte knew it was necessary. She told Edward, in as much detail as she could, what had precipitated the unlikely chain of events which had lead to the quarrel, including the fact that Edward's letter had unfortunately been the first link in the chain.

"I never would have believed it possible," Edward expostulated. "Jealous of your own brother?"

"Yes, I confess it took me rather by surprise, too," Charlotte admitted quietly.

"But Marwood must have known you better than that." Edward's gaze was frankly curious. "Surely he knew that you were not flirtatious by nature."

"Of course he knew it, Teddy, but he was jealous, pure and simple. You have to remember that Devon didn't know you were my brother that first time he saw us in the garden. He didn't even know that I had a brother. He simply found a letter that was signed, "my love always, Edward," and then right on top of it, saw you and I embracing. It's hardly surprising that he would jump to the wrong conclusion. I did, and on far less substantial evidence," Charlotte admitted sadly. "On the strength of a flimsy letter and a jealous woman's lies, I believed she was his mistress. The problem was, I was too proud to forgive him, even after he tried to explain the truth of the matter to me. And now that he's gone, it's too late." She bravely blinked back tears.

"Would that I had the chance to tell him how sorry I am."

"Now, Charlotte, you mustn't say that it is too late. We don't know that anything has happened to him," Edward said gently. "Look how long it took Osborne to get me out of France. You can't give up hope yet."

Charlotte nodded but refrained from commenting. She was all too painfully aware of having been in this position once before.

After breakfast, Charlotte wrapped a lacy white shawl around her shoulders and went in search of her aunt who, much to Dr. Palfrey's chagrin, was back to making her concoctions. She found her in the back kitchen, surrounded by a wondrous assortment of bottles and jars, little packages of dried herbs and of course, the ubiquitous Culpeper herbal.

"Good morning, Aunt Kittie."

Aunt Kittie glanced up from the packet of fenugreek she was labelling. "Charlotte, my dear, good morning." She came round the table to give her niece a kiss. "Are you feeling well?"

"Better, thank you, Aunt. Edward mentioned—"

"Did you take the camomile tea I sent up last night?"

"Yes, Aunt Kittie. He said—"

"Good. And the herbal tea this morning? Did you drink it all?"

Charlotte sighed. There was obviously no point in trying to proceed until her aunt had finished her interrogation. "Yes, Aunt Kittie, I drank every last drop, in spite of the rather strange taste."

"Never mind the taste. I put a drop of ginger tonic in it." Aunt Kittie cast a somewhat disturbed eye over her niece's too-slender figure. "Edward tells me you haven't been eating."

"Of course I have been eating."

"Not enough. Mrs. Bramble is most concerned about the amount of food you are sending back to the kitchen."

"Edward told me that you wanted to see me," Charlotte said, pointedly.

Recognizing the tone of voice, Aunt Kittie wisely decided not to belabour the point. "Yes, well, I wonder if you would be a dear and fetch some peppermint for me. Palfrey has told me that I am not to go outside until I clear up this little bit of congestion, but poor Lady Bering has been having some problems with her wind." Aunt Kittie chuckled. "Has been for years, but this is the first time she's admitted it. She's asked me to make her a tonic, but I have no peppermint at all. I think it is down by the—"

Charlotte smiled and turned towards the door. "That's all right, Aunt, I know where it is."

Charlotte picked up her basket and headed into the garden. The mornings were getting cooler now, reminding everyone that summer was coming to an end and that autumn would soon be upon them. She drew the cloak closer about her, shivering slightly.

What was Devon doing now?

She knew that Edward and Lord Longworth were in constant contact with Lord Osborne. She was also aware that the war department had sent another two men across to France in an effort to find Devon and Lady Duplesse, but all to no avail. The two men had managed to get back to England. Devon and Lavinia had not.

Locating the peppermint, Charlotte bent over her work, trying not to remember the angry words she had flung at Devon the last time they had been together. She endeavoured to forget the pain in his eyes and the anguish in his voice just before he had stormed out of the room.

Instead, she tried to remember that it was hope which had brought Edward home. A hope which had never faltered, no matter how bad things had become. Perhaps if she wished hard enough, hope would bring Devon back to her. Hope, and love.

When Charlotte had picked all the peppermint required, she started back up the path. Unbidden, her eyes went to the stone bench, and she paused, remembering the last time she had sat upon it. Suddenly, she was assailed by a wave of longing so intense that it brought an almost physical pain with it. She numbly moved towards the bench, recalling the way Devon had drawn her to it that day and proposed. She couldn't help but remember the way he had held her in his arms and kissed her, awakening a passion she had never thought to feel.

Charlotte sat down and pulled the cloak closer about her. She felt the damp coldness through her thin gown. The wind was picking up. Leaves swirled down and fell around her, settling like amber and russet jewels on a bed of green velvet.

She closed her eyes, and went back in her mind, remembering it all—the touch of his hands, the sound of his voice . . .

"Charlotte?"

She smiled. The voice in her dreams was so much like Devon's that the warmth of it flowed through her body like healing medicine. She willed the dream nearer, hugging it close to her.

"Open your eyes, Charlotte," the voice on the wind urged softly.

Charlotte felt her heart begin to pound. That was no dream, nor was it the wind. She squeezed her eyes tightly shut. "Spirit of the wind, do not tease me like this. If you are here, speak quickly, and say the words I long to hear."

"Open your eyes, my love. 'Tis no wind sprite you hear, nor figment of your imagination you see."

Charlotte's eyes blinked open, and she gasped. He was there in front of her, smiling down into her face, his beloved, familiar features a little haggard, but he was blessedly safe.

Charlotte did not even try to hide her tears. They flowed freely down her cheeks as she flew into Devon's arms, feeling the strength of his embrace drawing her close, pulling her against his heart.

There was no need for words; she told him all he needed to know with her eyes, with her hands and with her lips.

SOMETIME LATER, Devon sat on the stone bench with the woman he loved on his lap, and breathed a sigh of deep and utter contentment. Charlotte's dark hair flowed like water down her back, loosed from its pins by his searching fingers. He buried his hands in it now, loving the feel of the silky stuff against his skin.

She stirred happily in his arms. "I thought I had lost you," Charlotte whispered, her lips against the pulse in his throat. "I was so terribly afraid that I had lost you."

Devon smiled and hugged her closer. "I know, my sweet, and you will never know how sorry I am. I never meant to frighten you."

"Why didn't you tell me the truth before you left?" Charlotte asked softly. "After you had left . . . and Edward told me, all I could think about was the horrible way in which we parted—the terrible things I said—"

Devon pressed his finger against her lips. "Hush, Charlotte, there's no need to talk about that anymore. It's all over now. You're in my arms where you belong and everyone is safe."

Charlotte looked up into his eyes. "Madame Duplesse, too?"

Devon nodded, and brushed a kiss against her hair. "Yes, thank God, though there were times enough when I wondered whether she would remain that way."

Charlotte closed her eyes, unwilling to think about the dangers he had encountered. "How did you find her?"

"Through contacts. I still keep in touch with people throughout the countryside. They kept me pretty much informed as to Lavinia's whereabouts and eventually I was able to track her down."

Charlotte shuddered. "Poor woman. She must have been terrified."

"She was, but fortunately she is also very brave and resourceful. Lavinia told me that once she realized she had been spotted in the village, she started to head south, assuming that Boney's men would think she was making for the coast. That was what took me so long to find her. I had to travel much farther inland than I expected. Once I did locate her, I sent word to the captain of the ship that we would be at the coast by

ightfall. Unfortunately, when the French discovered
ur whereabouts I was forced to change our plans.''

Charlotte ran her fingers gently over his face. ''How
lid you get across the Channel?''

''By a stroke of incredible good luck. The captain
ent word to a friend of his down the coast that an
Englishman and his lady would be arriving within the
ext few days and to keep an eye out for them. I left
Lavinia with some people I knew I could trust and then
eaded up to the coast at Etretat, garbed as a fisher-
nan looking for work. I fully expected to have to
cratch out whatever arrangements I could. That's when
discovered Gaston already waiting for us.''

Charlotte's eyes revealed her concern. ''But how did
ou know that you could trust him, Devon? It might
ave been a trap.''

''Yes, it might have been,'' he agreed, ''but I've
earned to trust my feelings over the years, Charlotte.
Call it instinct, if you like. At any rate, we arranged a
ailing time and then I went back and got Lavinia. We
eft France that night.''

''And where is Madame Duplesse now?''

Marwood chuckled warmly. ''Enjoying a reunion
vith Lord Longworth not unlike this one, I should
hink.''

Charlotte glanced up into his dark eyes, and groaned.
Oh, Devon, I have been such an idiot. I doubted you
vhen I had no reason to. Can you ever forgive me for
ny own lack of trust?''

''I can forgive you anything, if you tell me here and
ow that you love me,'' Marwood said.

''I love you more than life itself,'' Charlotte told him
vithout hesitation. ''But I still feel such a fool. I real-

ize now that you were not seeing Lady Howard. I overheard her and Lord Barrymore talking at Lady
Rowallayne's ball. She was trying to make me think that
the two of you were having an affair."

"I know."

"You do?"

"I stopped in to see Celia on the way here. Your
mention of that rendezvous in the Park bothered me all
the time I was in France. I suspected before I left that
Celia was trying to make trouble, but it also occurred to
me that she must have had an accomplice. When I got
back and questioned Celia, she admitted that she had
coerced Barrymore into helping her. Barrymore had always had an eye for Celia, and after I insulted him at
O'Shaunessy's, it hardly came as a surprise to me that
he had thrown in with her. I am only sorry it didn't
dawn on me the first time you mentioned it."

Charlotte suddenly laughed. "I don't believe Lady
Howard and Lord Barrymore are seeing much of each
other anymore. She was not at all pleased with him that
night."

Marwood chuckled. "If that's the case, Barrymore
is luckier than he knows. I would not wish Celia on any
man."

Charlotte glanced at Devon, seeing the broad shoulders beneath the tailored jacket, the wind-ruffled black
hair curling around his collar, and knew what it was to
truly love. From the dim recesses of her mind, she suddenly heard the old Gypsy's voice. The Gypsy who had
predicted it all—the pain, the joy, and the letters—the
one in love's own hand by which she would be con

demned, and the letter by which she would condemn another. She had foretold it all, and it had all come true.

"I love you, Devon."

Marwood gazed down into her bright eyes and felt as though the sun had burst through on a cloudy day. He took one of Charlotte's hands in his and lifting it to his lips, pressed a long, lingering kiss into her palm. "Will you marry me, Charlotte?"

Charlotte's free hand lifted to caress his hair. "Just as soon as you can arrange it."

"My dearest Charlotte," he said, inadvertently quoting from the letter which had begun it all. Their lips met first in a whisper soft touch, a touch that deepened as the inevitable passion flared between them, banishing the memory of nameless doubts and replacing it with the forgiving warmth of love.

AUNT KITTIE, venturing into the garden a little while later in search of both her peppermint and her niece, spotted the pair of lovers on the stone bench and abruptly halted. They were so totally oblivious to anything other than themselves that her eyes blurred with tears. She quickly and quietly returned to the house.

"Well, did you find them?" Edward enquired with a broad smile.

Aunt Kittie fumbled for her handkerchief. "Yes, I certainly did."

"And?"

"It is no wonder Charlotte is taking so long. She is rather... occupied."

Edward bit back a laugh. "Was she indeed. And what about your peppermint?"

Aunt Kittie hastily wiped away a tear, and flipped to another recipe in Dr. Culpeper's book. "Lady Bering has waited this long for her tonic. She can certainly wait a little while longer!"

Relive the romance...
Harlequin®is proud to bring you

by Request™

A new collection of three complete novels every
month. By the most requested authors, featuring
the most requested themes.

Available in October:

DREAMSCAPE

They're falling under a spell!
But is it love—or magic?

Three complete novels in one special collection:

GHOST OF A CHANCE by Jayne Ann Krentz
BEWITCHING HOUR by Anne Stuart
REMEMBER ME by Bobby Hutchinson

Available wherever Harlequin books are sold.

1993 Keepsake

CHRISTMAS

Stories

Capture the spirit and romance of Christmas with KEEPSAKE CHRISTMAS STORIES, a collection of three stories by favorite historical authors. The perfect Christmas gift!

Don't miss these heartwarming stories, available in November wherever Harlequin books are sold:

ONCE UPON A CHRISTMAS by Curtiss Ann Matlock
A FAIRYTALE SEASON by Marianne Willman
TIDINGS OF JOY by Victoria Pade

ADD A TOUCH OF ROMANCE TO YOUR HOLIDAY SEASON WITH KEEPSAKE CHRISTMAS STORIES!

HX93

Fifty red-blooded, white-hot, true-blue hunks from every
State in the Union!

Beginning in May, look for MEN MADE IN AMERICA!
Written by some of our most popular authors, these
stories feature fifty of the strongest, sexiest men, each
from a different state in the union!

Two titles available every other month at your favorite
retail outlet.

In September, look for:

DECEPTIONS by Annette Broadrick (California)
STORMWALKER by Dallas Schulze (Colorado)

In November, look for:

STRAIGHT FROM THE HEART by Barbara Delinsky
(Connecticut)
AUTHOR'S CHOICE by Elizabeth August (Delaware)

You won't be able to resist MEN MADE IN AMERICA!

Calloway Corners

In September, Harlequin is proud to bring readers four
involving, romantic stories about the Calloway sisters,
set in Calloway Corners, Louisiana. Written by four of
Harlequin's most popular and award-winning authors,
you'll be enchanted by these sisters and the men
they love!

MARIAH by Sandra Canfield
JO by Tracy Hughes
TESS by Katherine Burton
EDEN by Penny Richards

As an added bonus, you can enter a sweepstakes contest
to win a trip to Calloway Corners, and meet all four
authors. Watch for details in all Calloway Corners books
in September.

HARLEQUIN CELEBRATES
THE SEASON OF SHARING
AND FAMILY WITH

Friends, Families, Lovers

Harlequin introduces the latest member in its family of
seasonal collections. Following in the footsteps of the popular
My Valentine, Just Married and *Harlequin Historical Christmas
Stories,* we are proud to present FRIENDS, FAMILIES,
LOVERS. A collection of three new contemporary romance
stories about America at its best, about welcoming others into
the circle of love.... Stories to warm your heart ...

By three leading romance authors:

KATHLEEN EAGLE
SANDRA KITT
RUTH JEAN DALE

Available in October, wherever
Harlequin books are sold.